Arse(d)

Mick Alec Idlelife

with foreword by Celia Micklefield

ISBN:13:978-1492325031

All characters and events in this publication are fictitious and any resemblance to real persons, living or dead, is purely coincidental.

DEDICATION

Dedicated to lovers of a.r.s.e. ends.

Considering there are so few of these words in the English language, their meanings crop up in people's lives with alarming regularity.

Mick Alec Idlelife 2013

CONTENTS

ACKNOWLEDGMENTS

I'd like to take this opportunity to acknowledge that I have been a pain in the arse during the creation of this book, which is probably appropriate bearing in mind its title. Learning to format for the various platforms has turned me into a howling monster from time to time.

I owe a debt of grateful thanks to family and friends for putting up with me. Some of them say they still love me.

Grateful thanks to Sue Johnson and her editorial 'hawk-eyes'.

FOREWORD
by Celia Micklefield

I think it might be because Mick was born in public that he became such a show-off.

It doesn't get much more public than the internet. Mick Alec Idlelife came into being in the full glare of the World Wide Web. If you'd been looking at the very moment that his alter-ego, Celia Micklefield was searching on Google, you might have witnessed the way the online anagram calculator churned up the letters of her name and discovered a brand new identity with a surname so irreverent and appropriate that Mick burst forth and sprang into life with a sardonic grin on his face.

Here was the answer to Celia's worries about writing in a different voice. Here was the means of letting readers of her women's fiction know *not to expect* a women's fiction kind of story.

Mick arrived fully developed. He didn't have time to grow up. His conception had been a performance of sorts and he continues to perform for audiences who appreciate his take on the vicissitudes of life. This is his first collection of short stories. Each is inspired by a word ending in the letters a.r.s.e. He likes to think Alan Bennet would approve.

(Alan Bennet doesn't know this. He is not responsible for what Mick thinks. I thought I should make that clear.)

P*ARSE from the Free Dictionary online -*
To make sense of; comprehend

TED. AND JUDY'S HOBBY

Chapter One

In the master bedroom at number twenty-nine Laburnum Grove, Ted puts on his new birthday tie.

Sixty today. A dark blue tie with little yellow teddy bears all over it.

'Are you nearly ready, Ted?' Judy is shouting. It sounds like she's in the kitchen. Pots are clattering. He can hear the oven timer pinging and there's the smell of pastry and eggs.

'Yes. I'm just putting on my tie.'

Sixty today and a tie with tiny yellow teddy bears all over it, kicking up their little legs, doing hand stands, wearing cutesy clothes and doing the gardening. Sixty today and another one of Judy's parties to look forward to. With another egg custard.

In the members' pavilion at the crown green bowling club, they'd be getting the first rounds in. They'd be gathering round the bar, having a laugh. His friend, Jim, from number eleven down the road would be tucking into his usual bag of pork scratchings that Mrs Jim never allowed when she was with him. There'd be pints of frothy, best bitter in dewy glasses, sparkling and cold, and a bottle of stout for Old Bob, the umpire. They'd be drawing up the new league and planning fixtures and there'd be a game of dominoes afterwards or maybe a few shots at the dartboard.

'Ted?'

'I'm coming.'

Ted stands in the doorway to the dining room and bites at his bottom lip. Judy has turned the room into Disneyland. Fairy lights adorn the walls and loop across the swags at the top of the curtains. Fluffy things they are, like blobs of cotton wool with stuck-on feathers. There's some sort of glitter stuff on top of the sideboard and sprinkled on the table. Fairy dust, Judy calls it.

Sixty today and fairy dust.

Twelve places are set for dinner. Fancy bows and curlicues are delicately etched onto the bowls of two wine glasses. There are two covers of the best silver-plated cutlery. There's Royal Albert English bone china in a design of pastel pink rosebuds and baby blue swags around the rims of two full-size dinner plates. Ten little tea plates in the same design perch on the fairy-dusted white cloth between child-sized knives and forks. Pink and blue ribbons decorate the handles of ten, tiny teacups. Two adult dining chairs. Ten antique high seats with wooden trays fixed in front.

'Light the candles will you, Ted?' Judy's voice comes from the hall. 'I'll just check on the littlies.'

Ted finds a lighter in a kitchen drawer. He can't quite believe what's happening again on his birthday, but soon the pretty blue and pink candles splutter into life inside their cutesy votives.

The front doorbell rings.

Here we go. Let's get it over with.

He opens the door. Judy is standing outside on the path.

'Here we are,' she says. 'Here we all are.'

She sounds excited and a bit breathless, as if she's rushed from somewhere, but it's all part of the game. She steps inside and removes her coat, which, Ted knows, she has only just this minute put on. He hangs it on a hook and then he helps her pull the old, *Silver Cross* pram over the threshold. The dinner guests, packed inside and dressed in their best waistcoats and bonnets, wobble about like little, furry drunkards.

'Here we all are,' Judy says again. 'Isn't this lovely?'

Ted follows his wife into the dining room where she parks the huge pram. She lifts out the dinner guests one by one and seats them in their high chairs.

‘Now, now, Barnaby. Be a good boy,’ she says. ‘No, you can’t sit next to Cuddles. Remember what happened last time you two sat together.’

Ted suppresses a groan.

Barnaby’s plush, teddy bear’s backside slips on his wooden seat and his chin hits the high chair tray. Judy tuts and wags a finger at him. Her generous behind jiggles in time with the finger. She props Barnaby up but he cockles over sideways.

‘Tell him, Ted,’ she says. ‘Tell him it’s best behaviour tonight. This is daddy’s special treat. Sixty today. Isn’t that something? It’s going to be lovely. Come to the table, Daddy. We’re all ready now.’

Ted takes his place as guest of honour.

Might as well just get on with it.

Sixty today.

He’s feeling every hour of it. He’s noticed, even without his readers, that his nose looks larger these days. So do his ears and yet the rest of him has shrunk, it seems. His trousers flap against lean shanks and he doesn’t fill his shirt collars the way he used.

Sixty today.

Judy’s not far off it, herself, but there she is with her hair held back by an Alice band and her lips painted too red. Her *Over the Rainbow* style frock, with its gathered up skirt and pinafore front, reminds him of a pantomime Dame, all bosom and ballast. He hopes that, at least, the food will be tasty. In any case, the guests won’t be eating any of it.

There are only the ten littlies around the table this evening, whereas, at one time, Judy would have struggled to decide which of the hundred and twenty four bears to invite. And the reason the dinner guests are so depleted is due to what happened the last time Barnaby sat next to Cuddles . . .

Judy was a talented seamstress. From a girl, she once told Ted, she’d taken a fancy to sewing things, cushion covers and aprons, embroidered tray cloths for her mother and grandma. At school she'd learned how to make her own dresses and skirts. She could run up curtains, too and had chosen fabric to make her own bedroom curtains when she was only thirteen.

A homely type, quiet and unassuming, she was the exact opposite of Ted's mother who couldn't ever apply her mind to putting a decent, hot meal on the table or looking to see if anything needed washing. Ted's mother was not designed for domesticity. Her interests lay beyond kitchen sinks, washing machines with electrically-powered wringers and gas ovens with eye-level grills, she said.

Ted often saw his mother staring out of the front room window, across the road and beyond the council houses opposite. Her gaze would wander upwards to the top of the hills and her expression was dreamy as if she was imagining Switzerland or somewhere equally pretty like Ted had seen in films, where there were blue lakes and bright parties of glittering people having cocktails on manicured lawns and talking about the state of the economy.

Ted's mother often told him she'd been born out of her time. Ted thought she'd been born in the wrong place. Industrial towns in the West Riding of Yorkshire didn't have a lot of glamour about them in the late 1950s when he was a child. Wrong time or wrong place, whatever, she would be off, out every night in her herringbone tweed skirt suits from John Lewis of Leeds and suede high heels from Russell and Bromley. With a snap of the metal clasp on her handbag, she'd disappear to some committee meeting for some good cause, leaving her husband and son to fend for themselves. It had come as a surprise to neither Ted nor his father when one night Mother went out to a meeting and never bothered to come back.

Judy was everything Ted thought he wanted in a wife. He couldn't imagine Judy would ever be interested in women's groups and joining committees. She hardly ever gave her opinion on anything to do with politics and current affairs.

‘Oh, well,’ she’d say. ‘I don’t really know.’ Or, ‘Oh, well. I’m not sure. What do *you* think?’

The pair had met in the queue for fish and chips outside Harry Ramsden’s after a coach trip to see Slik in concert, before the group went a touch punk and Midge departed. She wouldn’t let Ted walk her home.

‘No.’ she said. ‘I’ve come with a friend and I’ll go home with her, but thank you for asking.’

Ted had thought that a fine answer. That was the mark of loyalty. That showed a person who cared about others’ feelings. When the coach made the last drop, he trailed the two girls so he could find out where the object of his interest lived. He consigned the address to memory and on the long walk home, through dark, winter streets, he said it over and over in his mind to the rhythm of his footsteps. The soles of his shoes pealed against wet ironstone paving and the number and name of her street rang in his head. By the time he climbed into bed, it was like a song he wouldn’t ever forget.

There followed an exchange of brief notes before they met again. She wrote him she worked at the Skipton Building Society and Ted suggested he’d meet her on his Saturday afternoon off work at the council’s highways department. They could go to the cinema early showing.

They arranged to meet on the library steps, which was where most couples looked out for one another. Close to the centre of town and the central bus station, it was the ideal spot. Sometimes, of a weekend, there were more people on the library steps than ever went inside to borrow a book.

Ted joined the others waiting under the shelter of the porch over the steps. A fine Yorkshire drizzle was coming down from a March sky the colour of cigarette ash. Yorkshire drizzle could be fine and dense at the same time and Ted thought the old wives were perfectly correct when they said it gets you wetter than if it was pouring cats and dogs. The library steps were soon crowded as young men pressed closer to each other like penguins.

Ted smiled in a knowing way, as if he were an old hand at this waiting for a girlfriend on the library steps routine. It never occurred to him she might not come. He was one half of a courting couple now, flushed with pride, taking his new girl to the cinema and making those important early steps toward becoming a man. He breathed in sharply through his nose and stood tall. He stamped his feet against the shoes that were nipping and wondered whether he should light a cigarette to look casual, unconcerned, used to this hanging about on the library steps lark. He ran a hand through his hair and saw her coming around the corner. He didn't know how he was supposed to greet her so instead said,

'Good thing you brought an umbrella.'

Judy had on a new jacket. From C&A, she said.

'What do you think, Ted? Do you like it?'

He couldn't take his eyes away from her legs which were shrouded in wide, flared trousers. The combination of the tight jacket and flaring *loons* had the effect of cutting her in two, as if the top part of her body didn't belong to the bottom. But he said,

'Yes, it's very nice. I like the colour.'

She linked arms with him and they crossed the street, staying tight close to one another to share the umbrella. She took little strides compared with his own and her wide, wet pants wrapped themselves around his feet and shins. He was glad when they reached the comforting warmth of the foyer at the Ritz. He bought chocolates at the counter and presented the box to his girl. She smiled at him and he got that proud feeling again, the one that told him he was doing everything right.

The usherette showed them through the double doors and tore their tickets. The lights were up in the auditorium. There were plenty of seats free at the early evening showing. Judy led the way to a banquette on the back row.

Ted looked around to see if anyone was noticing. Everybody knew the back row was for courting couples. He felt he could burst with adulthood. He had crossed some invisible line now. He was somebody's boyfriend. Judy squeezed along the row, the voluminous fabric of her wide pants rustling as she moved. Ted settled in quickly beside her and tried not to think about what he imagined usually went on in the back row once the lights went down.

On reflection, *Rocky* had perhaps, not been the best choice for a first date, but Judy passed no comment and seemed content with her box of *Dairy Milk*. His arm slipped around her shoulder and she turned toward him. She leaned closer. He hoped his breath was fresh. She popped a *montelimar* in his mouth.

'I don't like those ones,' she whispered in his ear so close that her mouth brushed his skin. He hadn't expected that. His eyebrows shot upward all by themselves. The closeness of their bodies in the double seat on the back row and the whispering and the powdery smell of her, something like vanilla, and his arm around her shoulder and all that soft flesh beside him in the dark made him forget all about her baggy, damp loons and stirred in him a strong desire to get to know more about what was going on underneath all that fabric. He knew for sure what was rearing up underneath his own pants.

Size-wise, Judy was what Ted preferred to call cuddly. There was something wonderfully comforting about putting his arms around a girl who felt warm and soft with no bony bits and sharp angles. Her face was soft, too with eyes as trusting as a Jersey cow. Not so much of a delicate English rose, Judy was more of a rhododendron or a peony, blooming large and wide and hiding at the back of the garden.

It turned out her fulsome flesh was accommodating. Luscious and tender, it yielded to his touch on Fridays when his father was out, down the pub. She would get herself comfortable on the sofa and arrange herself so Ted could get a good look. He'd be there, on his knees on the fireside rug with one hand fondling her bits and the other rubbing at his own. He always wore two pairs of underpants on Fridays.

Fingering was all she would allow to begin with.

‘No, Ted,’ she would say when he asked if there was any chance they might move the physical relationship on a little. ‘No girl ever got pregnant by a lad’s finger. You’ll have to make do.’

And so, he made do. And he continued to make do, all the while hoping his persistence would win the day sometime soon.

‘Well, that’s what courting couples do, Judy,’ he’d remind her as he sank to his knees on the hearthrug by the electric fire on Friday nights. ‘That’s what love is all about, Judy.’

‘Is it?’

‘Oh, yes. I bet you’d like the real thing better than all this pretending.’

It was a brave shot and he’d timed it well. Her eyes were doing that fluttering thing and she was squeezing the muscles in her thighs. Her backside was juddering.

‘I’d have to feel more secure in where all this is leading, Ted,’ she said in little gasps.

‘I should think that will be all the way, Judy.’

‘And you love me?’

‘You know I do.’

They booked an overnight stay in Blackpool at a boarding house Ted had heard about from a work colleague. Judy told her mother she was staying with a friend. Ted met her at the train station and they ran down the platform holding hands just like all the honeymoon couples they’d seen on Saturdays.

They signed in as Mr and Mrs Noble and Judy giggled when Ted wanted to get her on the bed as soon as they were alone in their room.

‘What are you doing, Ted?’ she said, pushing back against him.

‘What do you think I’m doing?’ he said trying to manoeuvre her bulk back toward the bed.

‘That can come later, can’t it?’ she said. ‘We’ve got all the time in the world for that, Ted, love. Don’t you want to see what’s happening in the Tower Ballroom tonight?’

‘Not really, Judy,’ he said, thinking that something might happen in the region of his own balls if he didn’t offload soon.

‘They’ll know we’re not married if we don’t go straight back out, Ted.’

‘How do you mean?’

‘Married couples don’t start shagging as soon as they arrive somewhere, do they? Not when they can do it any time they want.’

Ted didn’t think it mattered what the landlady thought about their marital status. She’d have seen it all before. He tried to explain to Judy that Blackpool landladies would soon go out of business if they insisted on documentary evidence of their guests’ marriages, but Judy’s face was set and Ted didn’t want to spoil his chances for later. He’d waited long enough. A few more hours wouldn’t hurt and, by that time, he’d have made sure she’d had a couple of *Babychams* to help get her in the mood.

Her mood was giggly again by the time he had her on her back on the bed at Sea View Parade. He’d have liked a bit more appreciation of his efforts with the condom, but she seemed to think the whole procedure was a joke. When he asked her to lie back and open up, she enthusiastically obliged but she didn’t stop laughing.

They were an item now. Ted was invited to Judy’s for Sunday lunches and sometimes through the week after work for his tea. They called it *tea* at Judy’s house although it came at dinner time, or at the right time for *supper* as his mother had always referred to the meals she never made anyway.

Judy’s parents’ house was a proper home. They had a real coal fire with a half moon rug in front of it. The sofa was comfortably saggy and nobody minded if you rested your mug of tea on the chair arm. Judy’s father would sit, silently, in his favourite armchair, ignoring conversations, sometimes nodding to express his acknowledgement of Ted’s presence and every now and then getting up to change channels in the days before remote control.

On Sundays, there'd be roast sirloin and Yorkshire puddings that came up so big, they looked like a mountain range, with crispy outsides and soft, fluffy middles.

'This is brilliant! Just fabulous!' he said the first time he saw his plate put in front of him. 'I've never seen Yorkshire puddings like the Pennines before.'

'I made them,' Judy said with a coy smile, and if Ted hadn't already made up his mind about her, from that moment her fate was cast in batter.

He asked her on the quiet one Sunday night when spring had turned to summer and he was leaving to go home after two helpings of apple crumble, whether she might consider him a suitable husband. He used those exact words: a *suitable* husband. He'd seen a recent BBC costume drama and thought the phrase sounded just right. Elegant, but manly. Judy said she'd think about it and no more was said between them until the night, some months later when the clocks had gone back again, Judy brought the matter to a head.

'We could put our names on the list for one of them new council flats,' she said.

'Juday, Juday, Juday,' Ted said in his Cary Grant voice. 'No council flat for us. Oh, no. We'll buy our own house.'

Judy said he was funny and clever and her eyes sparkled like dew on a big, pink peony before Ted realised the enormity of what he'd said.

They began to save for a house deposit and Judy took up sewing things, for her *bottom drawer*, she said. They'd sit, round at Judy's with the television on and Mr Wilkinson snoozing in his armchair, while Judy embroidered pillow cases and her mother made a fresh pot of tea.

'You've got yer feet well and truly under that table, Ted,' his father said one Sunday as Ted was getting ready to go to the Wilkinson's for dinner. 'Best of both worlds you've got there, lad. Good luck to you.'

'I don't know what you mean, Dad,' Ted said.

'Getting looked after like that? And you still a bachelor? I haven't yet seen a ring on her finger. As I say, good luck to you.'

As he sat down to his weekday plate of shepherd's pie or a good beef stew at the Wilkinsons', Ted often supposed his mother would be having her *supper* with a different class of people now that she'd moved on. And good luck to her, too, he thought, remembering his father's words.

Life was good. A good life was a full stomach, enough cash in your pocket for a jar with the lads on your way home from work and a good woman not making too many demands on your time.

'This is very tasty,' he'd say to Judy's mum and Mrs Wilkinson would smile and say,

'Would you like some more, lovey? Judy, get Ted some more. The poor lad's been starved half to death most of his life. How's your father these days, Ted?'

And one day, Ted's answer was,

'He's joined one of them dating agencies. He says he wants to get married again.'

Judy's mum clapped her hands and said,'Well, that's a blessing is what I say.'

'How do you mean, Mrs Wilkinson?'

'Well,' she said, 'we thought he might have to wait three years for desertion. How come he got his divorce through so fast? What did you say, Judy? Irretrievable what? Never mind. It lets you off the hook, doesn't it, Ted? Now you don't have to worry about leaving your dad on his own. Judy, fetch that catalogue.'

And she leaned across the table and put her hand firmly on top of Ted's. 'You're free to set a date now, Ted,' she said, patting his hand with that same firmness. 'Not before time, love. Not before time is what I say. Judy, have you got that catalogue?'

Ted couldn't quite put a name to the unusual sinking feeling that dragged at his insides and ran down his legs when he saw what kind of catalogue they were talking about. His neck felt hot and he loosened his top button. He looked across the table to where Judy's father sat, silent as usual, stirring his pot of tea. The man was smiling. Only, it looked a bit sour, a curdled sort of smile like something gone off. Mr Wilkinson winked. Slowly. Very slowly. As if to say, you're in for it now, lad.

Ted looked on as Judy flipped the pages of the jeweller's brochure. She stabbed at one of the pictures with her finger.

'I like this one, Mum. Ted, come and look at this one.'

'A solitaire, Judy,' Mrs Wilkinson said. 'That's what you want. And twenty two carat gold, mind. None of yer cheap muck.'

She patted Ted on the shoulder. 'Well, you must be able to afford it by now is what I say. You must have saved a fortune by now Ted, love, eating round here nearly every day. A Christmas engagement! That's what we want.'

How imperceptibly the balance of power in a relationship shifts. On that night, with his plate of lamb stew and his rice pudding inside him and the New Avengers to look forward to on television, Ted was unaware that the tectonic plates of his existence had faulted around the dinner table at the Wilkinsons'. He didn't feel the free fall he was in. Rather, he was in a fog. If he wondered later how it was that his life had taken a sudden lurch in the direction of becoming the husband he'd really only hinted at wanting to become, he had not yet acquired the maturity it would take to recognise the fact that the day he told Mrs Wilkinson his father was going to be married again was the one defining moment of the beginning of the end of his own days as a bachelor.

When his head had cleared and he could see straight again, Ted looked up. Judy's father had his eyes closed. His fingers were wrapped around his mug of tea and his thumbs were circling one another. His mouth was still stretched in that sickly smile.

Ted's own mouth opened. It curled at the corners and then went a perfect square shape. He could taste something dry like bitter almonds on the back of his tongue. He couldn't feel his legs under the table.

Chapter Two

Ted didn't feel he was in his legs again until after the wedding ceremony in June. They were numb, as if they didn't belong to him. He couldn't put his finger on the exact cause but he was aware he wasn't firing on all cylinders. Feelings weren't getting through to his extremities. He'd wake up each day unrested, on edge, as if there were a riddle he'd been trying to work out all through the night instead of sleeping. The fog that had descended on him that night at the Wilkinson's dinner table had him in a cocoon.

He drifted from day to day in an unbalanced way. Sometimes, he wasn't sure how he'd managed to get himself to work in the mornings. It was as if he was operating on auto-pilot: his fingers fastened the buttons on his shirt without any input from their owner; his feet slid into his shoes the way a duck slips into the water and then looks surprised to be wet. He arrived at work, did what he had to do and drifted back home again.

At times, his father was at home; at other times, he wasn't. Ted's father had launched into an aggressive dating schedule in his own search for a wife. A *companion* is how he described to Ted what he was looking for in a woman. He actually had a checklist and once showed it to Ted, but through the fog in his eyes Ted paid little attention.

Months slipped by. Ted spent them in a haze of guest and wedding present lists and talk of bridesmaid fittings. Friday nights on the hearthrug went by the board, but when he complained about it Judy said it wouldn't be long before he'd be collecting his conjugal rights every night of the week if he wanted and not to be greedy now. Instead, he met with the lads on Fridays and settled into his position as fiancé, soon-to-be husband.

'Howzit going, Ted?' they'd ask him as they propped up the bar at the Lord Rodney. 'Still looking forward to tying the knot?'

And he'd answer,

'Oh, aye,' in a dreamy way. 'We've all got to grow up sometime.'

The happy couple moved into their semi-detached on a new estate after their June wedding and a honeymoon in Jersey. Ted was *in* his legs again. He was on a fresh footing. The ground felt firmer beneath him now he was a man of property. He knew where he was going. He wasn't just some kid aching to get his leg over. The fog had lifted. Ted felt he had purpose.

He returned to his work at the highways department in the local council offices as usual but carried about him an air of new, higher status: grown-up, married man. It made him throw his shoulders back and stand extra tall. When he sat at his desk, he did it with nonchalance, as if being a husband made him more of a man to be reckoned with. His half smile and the knowing twinkle in his eye spoke of a man who was getting it every night if he wanted it.

Judy returned to the Skipton Building Society a little tired from nightly shagging and being woken at three in the morning by a rampant Ted who seemed intent on making up for all the missed Friday nights. Sometimes, Ted was so unbridled he could do it in his sleep and didn't remember anything about it in the morning. Judy found that disconcerting. He might as well be humping a pillow case. She looked forward to the time when she could do the same as Ted and sleep through it. It would be much more convenient not having to respond. It wasn't as if they were making love to one another during those ruts in the dark. There wasn't much love about it at all. It was just humping. Sometimes she thought Ted had forgotten she was actually there.

'How was your day?' they would ask one another when they met in the Schreiber bridal kitchen after their day's work and then, rubbing his palms, Ted would ask as man of the house, eyes all bright with expectation,

'And what's for dinner tonight?'

Judy's Yorkshire puddings still rose like the Pennines, but she was a far cry from her mother when it came to turning out succulent roasts or thick, tasty stews.

‘Anyway,’ she’d say as she put out poached eggs on toast, ‘it’s summer, Ted. We don’t need all that heavy stodge. If you think about it, we don’t need so much of it through the winter, either. It isn’t as if we have demanding physical jobs.’

Ted thought all Judy needed was a little encouragement. Perhaps she lacked confidence. In any case, it wouldn’t be a bad thing if they both lost a few of the extra pounds they’d put on eating Mrs Wilkinson’s fare over the last eighteen months or so. He would bide his time. It couldn’t ever get as bad as things used to be when he depended on his own mother for sustenance.

They saw his mother, once, when he and Judy took a day trip to Morecambe. They’d bought nettle beer from a stall in Heysham and were walking back along the promenade for the last hour before the coach left for home when he saw her, his mother, strolling arm in arm with a tall man sporting a large moustache and wearing a cravat tucked in the neck of his country-check shirt.

‘Mother!’ Ted said.

‘Edward!’ she said.

‘This is my wife, Judy,’ Ted said.

‘This is my husband, Gerald,’ Mother said.

‘Come along, darling. We’re late already,’ Gerald said.

And Judy did something Ted never knew she had in her. As Ted’s mother and her new husband sauntered off, Judy ran after them and got in their way.

‘Call yerself a mother, do ya?’

Ted had no idea where Judy’s fishwife voice sprang from, or the jutting jaw and stance with hands on hips. ‘Call yerself a mother? A real mother feeds her son. She cares for him. Looks after him. She doesn’t walk out on him. Doesn’t just disappear into the wide blue yonder without a word or a by-your-leave. I’ll tell you what, though, lady. That was the best day of his life when you went, *darling*. Best day’s work you ever did, if you ask me.’

And Judy turned on her heels with her nose in the air. She linked up with Ted and held onto his arm.

‘Come along, *darling*,’ she said. ‘We’ll be late for *supper*.’

Supper that night was haddock and chips from Mosley's, the promise of a meat and potato pie the day after and the best sex they'd ever had. There was no giggling from Judy that night. She'd come away from the altercation with Ted's mother in a kind of euphoria. Walking on air, she was, like some twentieth century Boadicea, triumphant and vainglorious. She took charge of everything after her victory on the promenade at Morecambe. She marched into Mosley's and placed their order; marched Ted back out again for home. When they'd finished eating, she left the newspaper wrappings in a heap on the kitchen table and hurried Ted upstairs. She made him lie back on the bed and gave him his orders.

'Get it up, Ted,' she demanded, 'and you can forget the rubber.'

Number twenty-nine Laburnum Grove was a step up from the semi-detached on the Barratt estate. The Laburnums were among the most desirable addresses in town, the agent told Ted. Built between the wars for an emerging middle class who wanted mock Tudor beams and Charles Rennie Mackintosh windows, the Laburnums curved around an elongated letter S on a south-facing slope, overlooking the prettiest part of town where the river ran through parkland and trees, well away from industrial developments further along the valley.

Standing on a large plot, detached from other houses on the westerly cul-de-sac by stone walls all around, number twenty-nine, Laburnum Grove spoke of residents who were going up in the world. Laburnum Grove houses had double garages. Laburnum Grove driveways were longer and wider as were the two cars parked in them.

Ted's promotion at the Highways Department meant Judy could stop working. She had thrown herself into making new curtains with swags and tie-backs for their upmarket home. The business of moving house had raised her spirits, given her something positive to think about rather than dwell on the fact that after more than ten years of fish and chip suppers like the one after they'd been to Morecambe, there were no babies on the way.

'Never you mind, Judy, love,' Mrs Wilkinson said when she came to visit the Laburnum new home and her eyes were all over the place. 'Just look at what you've got instead is what I say.'

Mr Wilkinson grunted and actually spoke.

'Aye. Very nice,' he said when he was checking out the garage and Ted's new Granada estate car.

Ted's own father had little to say on the matter of neither the new house nor the want of tiny feet pattering, but the new wife on his arm showed a distinct dearth of understanding.

'Judy,' she said. 'I can call you Judy, can't I? I mean, I don't want you calling me mother-in-law. God forbid! No. You must call me Elaine. Now then, Judy. Do I look like anybody's grandma? You don't have to answer that. I'm telling you. I do *not* look like anybody's grandma. Truth be told, I don't ever *want* to look like anybody's grandma. Baby-sitting other people's brats is not on my list of things to do before I die. There now, I've said it. Now we all know where we stand, don't we? Did you say you'd got fresh ground coffee, Judy?'

Ted wondered why, in his search for his new *companion*, his father had trodden the same path as before.

'She's a bitch,' Judy said after the visitors had left. 'I felt like tipping her coffee right on the top of her over-bleached head. Her and that bloody awful coat. Chinchilla? Huh. Rabbit, Ted. That's all they are. Rabbits. I wouldn't mop the floor with it.'

Although Ted felt his Judy wasn't one day going to turn out *exactly* like her mother, there was something about the Elaine episode that pricked at his reasoning. Even though he'd felt a certain amount of pride that on the two occasions he'd seen her fly into a passion, she'd shown her true grit and stood up for what she believed in, he was nevertheless aware of an unusual discomfort in the pit of his stomach. While he congratulated himself on his choice of a fine, Yorkshire, big pink peony of a woman, he couldn't help wondering if he hadn't yet seen the full range of Judy's emotional manifestations.

He tried to imagine her mopping the floor with Elaine's fur coat, but instead of amusing him the image he conjured of Judy, on all fours, stretching out on the kitchen floor soured his stomach further. It would not be a pretty sight. Moreover, it seemed she was still expanding. And her voice was getting louder. She could present quite a formidable opponent if she chose, Ted thought.

Laburnum Grove was a quiet cul-de-sac. The people who lived in the house nearest were foreigners from somewhere over near Bolton so Ted and Judy had little to do with them, but there were other families who nodded and smiled and sometimes said good morning when they passed by.

It was Jim, from number eleven who was the first to invite Ted and Judy round for a barbecue. It took place on a Sunday afternoon and Jim's back garden was full of Laburnum Grovers, including the Bolton foreigners. There were children, too; girls sitting at a refectory table with colouring books and boys tapping a ball about. Judy sat with Ted on a garden bench.

'I didn't know there were children on the Grove,' Judy said to Mrs Jim as she came by with a tray of burgers.

'Oh, yes. They've all just come back from summer holidays. There's the Henderson's lad with Billy from number nineteen and over there's the two Waddington girls. This here's my nephew. Come over here, Rob, and say hello to Mrs . . . oh, heck, love, I don't know your name.'

'It's Judy. And this is my husband, Ted. We're at number twenty-nine.'

'Well, it's lovely to meet you both. I'll catch up with you again later. The kids are waiting for these burgers.'

Mrs Jim hurried off and all the kids gathered round her.

'What did she say her name was, Ted?'

'She didn't.'

'So, just Mrs Jim then, for now.'

'What do you make of that lot from Bolton?' Ted said.

Judy pulled a face.

'Funny accents they've got. Don't you think so, Ted? *She* can't talk properly at all. She says *chimley*. I heard her. And *lickle* instead of little. *Oh, what a lovely lickle play house,* she said when she saw Jim's Wendy house. I heard her say it. *Shall we get a lickle play house like that for when the lickle ones come to visit?* I tell you, it makes me cringe. I suppose when they get sick at their house they end up in *hospickle.'*

Judy grimaced and gnashed her teeth.

'Maybe she can't help it,' Ted offered.

'Lickle? Chimley? Hospickle? 'Course she can help it. Hey, I bet she can say shiT.'

It seemed a very long time since Judy had been reluctant to give an opinion, an age since she'd stared at him with those innocent eyes and said,

'I don't know. What do you think, Ted?'

Now, here she was all fired up about the way the Lancashire woman pronounced some words. Actually, when Ted came to think about it, Judy's reaction had sounded angry, bitter, a bit out of proportion to the alleged offence. But, he still tried to think of her as his peony growing out of that Yorkshire grit and when he noticed the way she was looking at the little girls with the colouring books, his heart melted for her. There was good reason for Judy to feel upset, he decided. Deep down, she was still soft and cuddly. He should try to bring that side of her out into the fresh air a bit more.

The lads at the Lord Rodney on a Friday night had stopped teasing him over his want of fatherhood.

'Wotsup, lad?' they used to say every week. 'Does tha' need a striker? Shall us come round and take it in turns?'

And he would laugh and go along with their jokes and teasing, but he'd had the tests and so had Judy. There was no medical reason they hadn't been fertile together. There was simply no answer. It just hadn't happened. Ted had resigned himself to the fact it probably never would. He knew Judy still hoped. He saw it in her eyes as she watched the two Waddington girls playing. He shouldn't be too hard on her.

They saw more of the Laburnum Grove children through the rest of that summer. Judy would send out plates of biscuits or call them in for ice creams when she saw them playing out. Sometimes, the Waddington girls brought dolls with them.

'This is Suzy,' the youngest said one day, 'but she's lost her knickers.'

'I'll make her some, if you like,' Judy offered. 'And her dress is looking a bit torn, love. Do you think she'd like me to make her a new one?'

It wasn't long before Judy was running up dolls' dresses and pram covers and full dress uniforms for the boys' *Action Men*. Ted saw how his wife blossomed again when she was making things for the children. The sadness was sometimes still there in her eyes, but it didn't come out of her mouth any more.

Judy had always been able to make something out of nothing. She was in her element now. She took scraps of this and that and turned them into outfits for the toys of all the neighbourhood children, including the ones from Laburnum Avenue round the corner, along the easterly curve of the Laburnums' elongated letter S. She made coats and jackets, skirts and trousers, shoes and boots. She even made cute little school bags with tiny rag books tucked inside. The dolls and soft toys of the Laburnums had never been so well dressed.

Then, one day, she made a Teddy bear. She called him Buster and he became mascot of the whole tribe of kids and toys. The children loved him to pieces, literally. They carted him around on their homemade buggies; they fed him worms and mud cakes; they strapped him onto the back of the Henderson's Labrador and pretended he was in the York races. When Buster was too torn and dirty to be fun any more, the children wanted a new one. Judy made three new Teddies and gave them away.

'You could sell those things,' Ted said.

'Do you really think so?'

'Make some more and take a stand at a craft fair, why don't you?'

So she did.

Ted went along to help set up. They'd visited the kind of thing before so knew what to expect. In the grounds of a stately home, marquees afforded shelter from inclement Yorkshire weather and inside the tents, plots were allocated and charged by the metre. You didn't get much space for your money, so you had to make the most of it. Ted borrowed a wallpaper pasting table from Jim and, together with his own pasting table and a couple of upturned crates, he built something Judy could throw cloths over to make the whole thing look like a shop counter. She prettied it up and draped it this way and that and by the time she'd set out the soft toys, Ted thought people would never know what was underneath the two dark green sheets from the sale at Marks and Spencer.

Before the craft fair was open to the public, a woman wandered over from her own stall of handmade birthday cards.

'How much are they?' the woman asked, fingering a bear in a blue waistcoat and matching cap.

'Ten pounds should cover it,' Judy replied.

'*How much*?' the woman repeated, her voice soaring to the top of the marquee. 'Here, love. You're new at this, aren't you? I can tell.'

She took Judy by the arm and drew in close, her mouth all puckered up and knowledgeable and her eyes like slits. 'Listen, love,' the woman continued. 'That's not enough.'

She led Judy across the grassy aisle to her own stand and picked up a birthday card.

'See this?' the woman said. 'Two pounds fifty.'

She picked up another and held it out. 'Three twenty five. How long do you think it takes me to make this, eh? Five minutes with a roll of sticky dots.'

It was a particularly pretty card with bits of ribbon and bows and a cute picture of a kitten in an old boot.

‘Well,’ Judy said. ‘I suppose you have to buy in your envelopes and your cellophane wrap.’

‘And printed labels and paper bags and stamps and inks.’

‘Hmmm,’ Judy said. ‘And all your other materials.’

‘Just have a look in the next aisle, love. Her with the oil paintings and him with the framed photographs.’ The woman leaned in extra close. ‘Oil paintings? You could squeeze it out straight from the tube and you wouldn’t be able to tell the difference. A quick slap, dash, that’s all *her* work is. Three hundred pounds, thank you very much. I wouldn’t give them house room. And the photographs? They’re all *black and white*! Go and see for yourself.’

‘I think I see what you’re getting at.’

‘Good,’ the woman said. ‘Now put up your price to twenty five, but before you do, lovey, I’ll have two for the twenty you were content to start out with.’

Judy agreed. She’d made her first sale. Ted baulked at the woman’s nerve, but couldn’t fault her business sense. He supposed he and Judy should be grateful for the woman’s input.

Judy’s Teddy bear designs sold like crazy. Ted and Judy discovered that once one person had stopped to take a closer look, other people would too. One customer attracted others like magnets. When there was a lull, Judy sent Ted to stand at the other side of the counter and pretend he was looking to buy. Then, they’d swap roles and Judy put on her coat to make it more realistic. It worked every time.

The birthday card woman came back at lunch time.

‘How is it going?’ she said.

‘I think I’m going to sell out,’ Judy told her.

‘See? What did I say? If your price is too low, people think there must be something wrong with the goods.’

Without fully realising the impact of what was happening, that this was the first step on a new path in their lives, Judy began her own business and Ted helped with the practicalities of booking stands at craft shows, packing up the back of their estate car and driving to and from weekend venues. He rigged up a simple lighting system so Judy's Teddy bears sat under the spotlights on their cushions and in their baskets. With striped waistcoats and with bodies gleaming in the lights they looked like A-list celebrities.

At the Christmas fairs, Judy gave the bears miniature Santa hats and tied plastic holly on the lighting rig. She bought in special carrier bags and put fairy dust inside them. At Easter, she had girly bears in Easter bonnets and decorated the stand with rockery plants and mini eggs in birds' nests made from straw.

Over the course of the next ten years the price rose from twenty five pounds to fifty five pounds. Judy's name was known beyond the marquees of country craft fairs. She had a reputation for creating the finest and cutest soft toys. She set on the Waddington girls' mother and another woman from the Avenue. They sewed together the body pieces Judy had cut for them, but Judy made all the heads herself.

'It's all done with love,' she told Ted when he asked why she took on so much work. 'Nobody loves these bears like I do. That's why they have such adorable faces.'

Ted was beginning to find the bears not all that adorable all of the time. For one thing, their bits and pieces were spreading through the house and whenever she came up with a new design, like the Valentine bear and the Best Mum in the World bear, Judy would refuse to let the prototype go.

'Those ones are not for sale, Ted,' she'd say. 'They're like my babies, do you see? I gave birth to those ones. They stay with me. Always.'

What was more, Judy spent so much of her time sewing, getting ready for the next show and meeting her orders that Ted couldn't remember the last time he saw a nice, big square Yorkshire pudding like the Pennines.

One day, when he was the wrong side of fifty, Ted came home with a sour face. His skin was pale and there were dark rings of worry under his eyes. He didn't say to Judy *how was your day?* He didn't even ask what was for dinner. Judy followed him into the sitting room where he slumped into a chair after he'd removed the prototype hoodie bear that was sitting there.

'What's the matter?' she said.

'I can't believe it. I've been made redundant. I'll never get another job at my age.'

So, it was a good thing, Judy said, that the price of her creations had soared to nearly two hundred pounds. They were collectors' items now, dressed in the best fabrics and stuffed with laboratory tested, EU accredited materials so they could carry the official tag. Each bear came with its own adoption certificate, signed with a flourish by the maker herself.

'Don't fret, Ted,' Judy said. 'You know we'll manage. Anyway, you were getting fed up of all them new procedures at the council and targets and stuff. And what's it called? Health and Safety? You don't have to worry about it now, love. You can find something else to do.'

Judy went off to make a cup of tea. Ted attempted to summon up some vestige of pride in his wife's enterprise. She worked hard; you couldn't deny that. Credit where credit was due. Even though he'd lost his own job, there'd still be enough money coming in to meet all their bills, except that now it would be money Judy was earning, not him. On the downside, he'd have too much time on his hands till he found employment. Judy might expect *him* to make the dinners. On the upside, he could offer his services down at the crown green bowling club, maybe apply for vice president or treasurer.

He picked up the hoodie bear and put it back on the armchair. It looked like that Henderson boy when he used to charge up and down the Grove on his mountain bike. It even had the same cheeky expression on its furry face. He was working out in Thailand now, the Henderson boy. Fresh out of university and calling himself an executive something or other. Nice. The Waddington girls all grown up, too. Having babies of their own.

There wasn't really anything to worry about. He should count himself lucky. There were worse things could happen than share your home with Teddy bears. Only, he couldn't help wishing there weren't so many of the furry, little cuties sitting about the house in their bright new clothes and with their EU accredited eyes following him wherever he went and whatever he did.

Chapter Three

Judy was already using the two spare bedrooms for her sewing business. Both rooms were filled, packed to the gunnels. In one, floor to ceiling shelves that ran from wall to wall overflowed with fabrics and threads, Teddy bear heads and paperwork. The other bedroom housed her work table and there were filing cabinets lined up against two walls, filled with files and invoices. She said she needed a sort out.

'To be honest, Ted,' she said, 'I really need a separate office. I can't go on like this.'

He knew what was coming next.

'I'll move my things,' he said.

'Will you? Thank you, Ted.'

And she rushed off to begin. Rather, she jiggled. Sitting down at her work all day had considerably broadened Judy's beam. Her upper storey was in the same state of development, Ted noticed as he watched her retreat, her upper arms wobbling to the same rhythm as her backside. He stifled a sigh and went to his office.

The office downstairs had been Ted's own space. His den. His sanctuary. It had been the one place he could get away from the radio or the television when he came home from a frustrating day at the council offices, needing peace and quiet to unwind and stretch the knots out of his neck. More, since Judy had started her sewing business, he could shut the door to his home office and not hear so much of her machine whirring and stopping, whirring and stopping. Sometimes, the predictable rhythm of Judy's sewing machine noises hammered in his head like an ancient method of water torture, but instead of a constant drip, drip, plink, there was a blurred sort of sound like muffled drilling, then silence, followed by more muffled drilling, drumming on the carpet in the back bedroom, reverberating through the ceiling above him. As he made himself a cup of tea when he got in from work, Ted would wait for the stop, wait for the start, then wait for the stop and start of it again. On, off. On, off. Maddening. In his den, he could close the door on it. He could escape.

He'd hurry indoors, make his tea, close his office door and sit in his crumpled leather armchair to catch up with the daily newspaper. It was his down time, comforting and precious, when he felt he was regaining his equilibrium with his cup of steaming tea and cushions underneath him and at his back to counteract the slipperiness of the leather seat. He'd read the sports pages and maybe do a crossword and there'd be the smell of his supper cooking drifting along the hallway.

Since he'd been made redundant he had all day to read the paper and, therefore, to be honest, no real reason to object to Judy using the office for her business. The trouble was, he also had all day to listen to that whirring and stopping. Where could he go to get away from it? He thought about spending more time in the members' pavilion at the crown green bowling club. He could mix with the others a bit more, make himself known, make his presence felt before he'd let it be known he was interested in joining the committee.

The thought jolted him. Interested in joining the committee? He remembered his mother, in her tweed suits and suede high-heeled shoes and the way she couldn't wait to get out of the house. He wondered, briefly, what it was she needed to get away from all those years ago. His father? Himself? It was strange, he thought, how history seemed to repeat itself and one generation did exactly the same as the one before.

Judy took over the office downstairs in a matter of hours. She had it planned like a military manoeuvre. She had cartons and boxes packed and stacked and lined up with the precision of a task force in the hall and on the landing before he'd even finished thinking about where he was going to put his own belongings.

'I won't need that old chair, Ted,' she said.

'But, I thought you'd want it for your office.'

'Well, I did at first, but you know what? I've changed my mind. I think your old office will work better as my sewing room and the paperwork can stay upstairs.'

'You're going to do the sewing downstairs?' His mouth dried suddenly.

'Yes. It makes more sense. When I'm upstairs, I can't hear the radio.'

'We could put one up there.'

'No spare socket.'

'I thought you liked working upstairs out of the way. I mean, where you won't be disturbed.'

'It disturbs me every time I have to come down to make a cup of tea, and don't say we could put a kettle up there. And then, there's the phone. It's nearly always somebody wanting to speak to me. No, Ted. I'm going to work down here. Where it suits me. It's not about you this time, is it?'

Ted's stomach sank. His den, his sanctuary very swiftly became Judy's sewing room. He emptied his shelves, threw away a lot of his back copies of trade magazines and made a pile of books for the charity shop. He moved his slippers and lifted off his old jacket from the hook on the back of the door. He tried it on. It was too big. It made him look older than ever, with its great, wide shoulder pads hanging off him. He hadn't realised he'd lost weight. When had that happened? How was it he was shrinking, but Judy was growing bigger still?

He went through the drawers and found things he'd forgotten about: an old photograph of his father wearing a jacket that looked as big on him as the one Ted had just put in a black, plastic bin bag. He gathered up all the pens and pencils and chucked them in a box for sorting later; he saved unused scrap pads and dawdled about, reading some of his old work notes before dumping the rest. His notes for upcoming meetings and the like were easily shed. He had never for one moment missed those anxious mornings with all the department heads present, all with expressions like hawks looking to score points at others' expense.

But, he didn't want to part with his comfy, leather armchair. It would be like casting off an old friend, or taking a loved family pet to be put down. He couldn't do it, but the chair had nowhere to go inside the house. He wheeled it through the hall, out the kitchen door and into the garden. He kept going, around the back of the house and, through the rear garden door, he lifted his old friend into the workspace at the back of the garage. The chair looked forlorn, sitting there on the concrete floor all by itself. Surrounded by shelves of tools and tins of all his DIY bits and pieces, clamps and power drills and the like, his beloved chair was out of place and unnecessary. He knew how that felt.

When he went back to the house, Judy had removed his old shag rug from her new sewing room and put it with the pile for waste disposal. There were years of wear left in it. He didn't want to simply throw it away. He picked it up and took that out to the garage, too. He pushed his chair to one side while he spread out the shag rug. He had to put it at an angle to fit the space, sort of on the diagonal rather than square on as it had always been in his office. It looked different, almost new. When he put his chair back on it, what had been an empty space now looked quite inviting. He took a step back and regarded the arrangement.

Here was his answer. Here was where he could go to get away from the noise of Judy's sewing machine and Radio Two. He felt a smile stretch his mouth. A warm feeling ran through his belly. It could work reasonably well through the summer. With the door open, he'd have a view of the garden. He'd be able to sit here with his newspaper and keep an eye out for cats sneaking up on the bird bath.

He fastened back the rear door and sat facing the doorway to try it out. He tapped out a little rhythm with his toes. If he cleaned the small window thoroughly, there would be more daylight coming in on days when he had to keep the door closed. Winters would be a problem, though. He stopped tapping and began to make serious plans.

All he needed was a portable heater and a little table with a lamp on it and he'd have his own, private sitting room. Somewhere to get away all year round. His new escape. His private time. His toes tapped out a more determined rhythm. It was decided. He was going to make it happen.

He got up and stood, gazing out at the garden. The shed in the bottom right hand corner could look attractive with a bit of trellising round it. It could be an even better hidey-hole than the garage if he rigged up power and plumbed water down there.

A project! He had new purpose. He flopped into his chair, his mind suddenly clear. The garage would be his temporary apartment until he made the shed ready for occupancy.

***

'In the garage?' Jim asked Ted in the members' lounge on their regular Friday Happy Hour at the bowling club. 'You go and sit in the garage?'

'Until the shed's ready. I can't stand the constant noise in the house, Jim. I can't tell you how much it gets to me. That and the radio all day long. It does your head in. It's worse than a pneumatic drill.'

Jim made a whistling noise and shook his head.

'You need to get out a bit more. It's good to have a project with your shed and all that, but you've got to take time off, away from it,' he said. 'Carry on like this, lad, and you'll make yourself proper poorly.'

He picked up his pint and took a good drink. Ted followed suit. He pondered on Jim's advice for a moment and said,

'What do you do since you retired?'

'Me?' Jim said. 'I sit in the garage or the shed.'

It was Jim's turn to drive. Ted suggested they stop on the way home for a kebab. A few pints always gave him an appetite and Judy's dinners didn't exactly fill him up these days. She said she didn't want big dinners any more, but he knew that was because she was munching on biscuits, cake and chocolate all day long. He'd seen the empty wrappers in the kitchen waste bin.

The kebab shop was right next to the supermarket. Jim parked at the far end of the late night shoppers' car park and they sat, eating and watching people come and go.

'I wouldn't go in there on a Friday night if you paid me,' Jim said. 'Look at it. It's a bloody nightmare.'

Ted took another bite of his kebab and chewed slowly while he looked through Jim's windscreen and thought of a response.

Couples and families, trolleys piled high, noisy little kids in the seats at front, bigger, noisier kids hanging onto the side, car boots opening, closing again with a bang, trolleys back to the bays, cars coming in circling around for a parking spot nearer the entrance, cars going out, cars reversing, brake lights and headlights, and more trolleys and more people and queues at the cash points and the lights from the store and the entrance doors opening with a swish and closing, opening, closing, swish.

'Do you think we're getting past it, Jim?'

'Past it? I've passed it and come back round behind it, lad. I'm lapping it, Ted. I'm lapping it.'

Ted ate slowly, making it last. He didn't want to go home. He dreaded walking through the door to find Teddy bears and their belongings filling every seat, sitting on every horizontal surface, cluttering the hall stand, staring at him as he came in, as if he had no right to be there. They made him feel ill. They were like a furry, yellow pandemic spreading all through the house. Most of all, he hated passing his old den if Judy was in there, still working with the door open.

Teds, in various stages of completion, filled the floor to ceiling shelves. They all seemed to be looking at him, watching him with their beady, EU accredited eyes, as if to say, *what, you again*?

But what could he do about it? After all, Judy was the breadwinner now and needed the space more than he did. All the same, he was glad when she kept the door closed. It could be disconcerting seeing those spare limbs lying about. *And that box of eyes?* All different sizes to fit the range of bears she was making now. The big ones were the worst, lying there looking up at him. Hundreds of accusing, headless eyes staring out of a cardboard box. He couldn't look at them.

'What's up, Ted? You've gone quiet.'

'I don't know where to begin,' Ted said as he let go a sigh. 'It all sounds so stupid.'

He screwed his kebab paper into a tight ball. 'She's bought a high chair, Jim.'

'Who for?'

'The bloody bears. She's going to have them sitting round the table with us at mealtimes. It's getting ridiculous, Jim,' he said. 'They're all over the bloody place. I can't sit down to watch a bit of telly without a sofa full of bears beside me. I tell you, Jim. They're everywhere.'

'She never had any kids of her own, did she?'

Ted shook his head.

'So think yourself lucky, then.'

'How do you mean?'

'Well,' Jim said, 'if she didn't have all them toys to baby, she'd be babying *you*.'

Bearing this in mind, Ted was able to carry on for a while. The thought of Judy fussing and faffing round him in the same way she fussed over the bears was enough to set his teeth on edge. She'd changed, it seemed to him. Somewhere along the line through their years together, the pretty peony had been strangled by a stronger, more voracious variety with its tendrils creeping right through the house, budding into a new, yellow furry friend wherever the thing latched on. If he sat still long enough, the things would start growing on him, too, or maybe burst out of him like the alien in that film. There they'd be, covering him, smothering him. Choking the life out of him.

He tried to apply Jim's advice. He perfected the art of squeezing past the enormous *Silver Cross* pram in the hall. Packed with Teds in their outdoor clothes, it was like a throwback to the fifties. He could remember seeing prams like that parked outside houses near his childhood home. Enormous things, they were. No wonder they were left parked outside. Judy insisted on keeping hers inside, though. She said it was vintage, almost an antique and she polished it till the spokes gleamed.

Ted taught himself to ignore the little Ted that stood guard over the toilet roll. Judy didn't think it in the least embarrassing. Ted thought such whimsies entirely inappropriate for a woman Judy's age. It was sad. It was sick. Cringeworthy.

He grimaced at the tiny one inside the biscuit barrel with a notice in its paws that said: *190 calories each.* He could live with the bank of Teds that occupied the conservatory, lined up like Russian dolls on the cane work sofas, biggest at the rear with smaller ones in their laps.

He disregarded the one that carried the television remote in its backpack. He looked away when Judy set out a child-sized patio table and chairs in the back garden so the bears could have their own picnics when Ted brought out the barbecue.

But, when the little buggers moved into the bedroom, his patience expired.

'In the bedroom?' Jim said at the bowling club trophy presentation evening. 'What? Actually in the bed? Nay, lad. That's a bridge too far. You'll have to tell her to get rid of some of them.'

When, on the occasion of his fifty-ninth birthday, Ted had had to share his favourite meal with one hundred hand-sewn snouts and pairs of piercing plastic eyes, he could stand it no longer. He laid down his knife and fork, slapped his hands on the table and said,

'You'll have to get rid of some of these bloody bears, Judy. They're driving me mad.'

Judy raised a finger to her lips.

'Shush,' she said, her eyes all soft and dewy. 'Don't let them hear you say things like that. Poor Cuddles. Look, you've upset her.'

Ted watched his wife lean over and caress the female bear sitting next to Barnaby. She fluffed out its frilly frock and adjusted the bow behind its ear. Then she kissed it. Ted's stomach roiled.

'She's pregnant, Ted,' Judy said. 'Twins. And Barnaby's the father.'

She was looking straight at him. Her eyes had lost the softness; now they were hard and piercing as the bears'. He knew she was challenging him.

'Don't be so bloody stupid, Judy. You've gone too far this time. It's not right. Anybody would think you'd gone wrong in the head.'

'It's you who's the fool, Ted,' she said, and her voice had a bass undertone loaded with a threatening something he'd heard somewhere before. 'What gives you the right to sit there and tell me what I can and can't do, eh? You, who does bugger all around the house. You, who hasn't lifted a finger to make me so much as a sandwich in the last eight years you've been off work. You, who slopes off to that old man's park at the least excuse. Call yerself a husband, do ya?'

His face felt hot and there was a stab of consciousness that his whole life had been leading him to this moment, that his courtship of Judy, his marriage to her and his efforts to make her happy had been like a prologue to the real story, the starter before the main dish. This was the meat of it now. This was the main course. This was where the whole thing culminated and would define the nature of the dessert to come afterwards. As sure as day follows night, he thought, the dessert this time would not be the best sex they'd ever had.

Ted had acquired the maturity now to recognise those defining moments when they presented themselves. He steeled himself for further confrontation. He understood the look of determination in Judy's eyes when she said,

'We'll be able to have another christening party soon. Won't we?'

Her question hung over the table between them. This was it, then. Here it was: the defining moment. He stuck out his chin.

'Judy, I've had enough. Get rid of some of them.'

She stood up and glared at him.

'I will never, repeat *never* get rid of any of my bears. How could you say such a thing?'

It was Ted's turn to stand.

'Because I *am* your bloody husband, Judy.'

She put her hands on her hips.

'And?'

He made for the door and his parting shot was,

'I mean it, Judy. It's me or the bears.'

He felt quite calm as he got in the car and pulled out of the drive. It was remarkable how peaceful he was. As he drove away, he searched himself for a feeling he could put a name to, but he wasn't angry. In fact, he felt cool, composed. Undisturbed. There was none of that nervous sensation he used to get sometimes at the council offices when the buck stopped with him. He flicked on the car radio and cruised along. His head was clear. His conscience was untroubled. He'd delivered his ultimatum to Judy and he was going to stand by it. It was as simple as that. He was going to take back control.

He smiled. Jim would be at the bowling club. He wouldn't mind staying out a bit later than usual. They might even stay till closing. Coming home extra late would underline his determination to reassert himself at home.

At the bowling club it was the guest beer night. Management had booked a turn, a band doing covers of seventies songs. The music was thunderous. As soon as Ted stepped inside, it blasted in his ears like a punch in the face. His lip curled and his insides heated up. The drumbeat was loud and insistent, the voices strident and jarring. He felt his equilibrium slipping away. In seconds his composure was stripped from him. He felt violated. Robbed.

He found Jim and Old Bob, the umpire, up at the bar. They were just about to order.

'I'll get these,' Ted shouted over the racket. 'What's with that bloody awful music?'

'Committee decision, Ted, lad,' Jim shouted back. 'Just to see how it goes down with the members. They're thinking for social evenings and such like, it might attract more of the wives in.'

'Tell 'em not to bother,' Ted bellowed. 'What did they want to go and do that for? I come here to get away from all that. Anyway, it's a bowling club, not a bloody working men's. They'll be bringing in Bingo next!'

They found a table as far away from the loudspeakers as they could get.

'I take it the bricks are still falling down at home,' Jim said.

'Something like that.'

Old Bob poured his stout and took a long drink.

'Is she still making all them toys?' he said. 'Didn't they do a piece on her in the Yorkshire Post not long since?'

'She is and they did,' Ted said. 'Bob, if you don't mind, that's the last thing I want to talk about tonight.'

'Why? What's up?'

The whole lot came out: the Silver Cross pram, the full sofas in the conservatory, the toilet roll fiasco, the biscuit barrel, the Teddy bears' picnic table and chairs, the buggers on the blanket box in the bedroom and Judy's latest purchase of a high chair. Ted spilled the whole sorry tale. He unburdened himself.

'How many did you say?' Old Bob said.

'At the last count, a hundred and twenty four.'

'Bugger me,' Old Bob said and sucked through his teeth.

'She's stopped cooking him proper dinners as well,' Jim added. 'He's living on chips and kebabs.'

The old boy sucked louder through his teeth.

'Well, I know what I'd do,' he said.

'What?'

'Get shot of some of 'em yourself, Ted. With all that many lying around, I bet she'd never even notice.'

And so, Ted planned his first murder.

Chapter Four

Ted lay in bed and considered what he'd done. Judy was asleep beside him, on her side, facing away from him as usual. She always fell asleep quickly, as did he before he became a killer. He'd always slipped into slumber easily, readily, welcoming the drowsy floatiness that came before that last conscious moment when he knew he was going under and he would stretch out to switch off his bedside lamp. Now, he lay feeling Judy's warm bulk at his back, but sleep was keeping its comforts from him. His heart was cold and murderous, keeping his mind awake and his eyes open.

He let his head sink deeper into his pillow and stared at the ceiling. His mouth stretched into a thin grin. Disposing of the first four little ones had been a simple matter. Ted had waited until Judy closed the door to her sewing room and then pretended he was going out to the garage. He deliberately made a lot of noise as he turned the key in the lock and went in. Then, he crept back out again, wearing his old slippers and, moving on tiptoes, slinked into the house. He could hear the whirr, stop, and whirr, stop of Judy's sewing machine. He sneaked into the conservatory, nabbed two tiny Teds from the windowsill and took them to the kitchen. He rolled them up in old newspapers, carefully so as not to make rustling noises and slipped outside to put them in the wheelie bin. A few days later, he did it all again. Old Bob was right. Judy didn't notice.

He lay with his bedside light on low, listening to Judy's sleeping noises. The grin disappeared from his face. His jaw fell slack and his bottom lip went pouty. In fact, he wasn't at all happy. The thought troubled him. He wondered why he didn't feel elated. He'd managed to get rid of four of the little buggers. He should be on top of the world. He should be like a kid who'd snatched the last doughnut. He ought to be full of the joys of his success.

But it wasn't enough. There was no satisfaction in it. Ted wanted a proper murder, a gut-spilling, ear-splitting affair with gouged eyes and fluff all over the place. Not in the house, though. No. Fluff all over the place, Judy would notice. The deed would have to take place elsewhere. He began to plan his next moves and found himself grinning again. He grinned until drowsiness prompted him to stretch out and turn off his bedside light. His fingers made monster shadows on the ceiling as he reached for the switch.

Ted enjoyed the planning of his next few murders. It gave him the sense of satisfaction he'd been craving to know that while Judy was busily sewing away in his old den, he was selecting his next victim and the means of its disposal.

He dispatched the one called Eric in the garden shed and stuffed him in small pieces in the watering can he used for weedkiller. He poured more chemicals on top of the mangled, furry bits and the resulting sulphurous whiff was agreeably evil.

Felicity hung herself from the shed rafters with the ribbon from her own Easter bonnet. Ted slashed at her with a screwdriver as she swung there, her innards spilling at his feet.

One day, when Judy was out shopping, Clive got it in the neck on the breadboard and the bread knife made a fascinating rasping noise on the bear's collar. This was more like it, Ted thought as he wrapped Clive's remains and hid them in the boot of his car. On his way to the bowling club, he stopped and dropped the decapitated Clive in somebody else's rubbish bin.

Jim laughed when Ted told him how much he was enjoying himself.

'How many's that you've done in?' he said.

'Seven.'

'Why don't you bring one round to mine?' Jim said. 'We could do one together.'

'I've got a better idea,' Ted said and his mouth twisted into a lopsided smile.

They planned a *hit*. A Ted-napping to coincide with the October annual general meeting at the bowling club. That way, Judy and Mrs Jim would expect the menfolk home late. Ted and Jim would be able to make the most of the occasion and take their time over it. It would need careful planning. Ted was going to go for one of the big ones.

The weather turned out perfect for it: a steady drizzle and night that fell early with the street lamps doing that fuzzy, halo thing. Ted lifted the bear from its place on the blanket chest in the bedroom and stuffed it under his raincoat.

'I'm going now,' he called to Judy who was still working in her sewing room. 'Don't wait up. I'm planning to have a few pints with Jim.'

The sewing machine noise stopped and the door opened. Judy popped her head out.

'Okay,' she said. 'I should finish this commission tonight, if I keep at it. Then I'll probably go straight to bed. Have a good time.'

She closed the door and the sewing machine started up again. Ted wondered about Judy's latest commission. She'd been working on the same piece for a long time, it seemed to him. The pieces of fabric were much larger than usual. Maybe it was for an exhibition.

In the garage, Ted duct-taped the bear's snout and tied its paws together. He covered the eyes with a blindfold made from one of his old ties. For good measure he secured a plastic bag over the bear's head. Then, he hid it in the boot. He turned out of the drive to Billy Joel's *The Stranger* on the car's CD player and he whistled along as he made for Jim's house further down Laburnum Grove.

Jim came running out like a kid from school. He launched himself into the passenger seat.

'Is it . . .?' he said.

Ted nodded toward the rear of the car.

'Don't say any more about you know what,' Ted said.

'What's that music, Ted?'

'Everything's in order, Mr White. Fasten your seat belt. We don't want to draw attention. And call me Mr Black.'

'You what? Oh, I get it.'

Jim wriggled into his seat, then affected a straight face. They travelled the rest of the journey in silence, except for Ted's whistling to the music and the clicking noise from the CD as he hit the replay button. *The Stranger* was the perfect accompaniment, Ted thought. Not the right music from the film *Reservoir Dogs*, but the atmospheric whistling of Joel's composition sounded like spies in Vienna and lonely city centres with lots of dark alleys and mysterious figures hanging around street corners. They cruised along the wet streets of the town centre with its shops all closed and dark. By the time they reached the club Jim had learned the melody and they got out of the car, both whistling and with their coat collars turned up.

Mr Black and Mr White went to their meeting as calm and composed as you like. They voted in the new president and treasurer as if nothing was amiss while all the time the hapless victim lay bound and gagged in the boot of Ted's car outside on the gravel car park, cold and unloved. And dead.

Lucky, the bear, dismembered, disemboweled and decapitated over a couple of pints of best bitter, went into the compost heap round the side of the club house, a wooden, pavilion-like structure which backed onto the river. Ted and Jim drank to their success under a starless sky and by the sound of inky water rushing over the weir.

'Hey, we could do a drowning next,' Jim suggested. 'I know a really good place further down the river bank.'

Finally, Judy confronted Ted. When she appeared in the doorway of Ted's sanctuary in the garage where he was sitting with his coffee and newspaper, his plans for renovating the garden shed temporarily on hold, he knew by the look on her face that the game was up.

'I've just been looking for Esmerelda,' Judy said. 'It's time she had her underwear changed. I've looked everywhere, Ted, but she's nowhere to be found. Now, what do you think about that? Is there anything you'd like to tell me, Ted? Ted?'

He gulped at his coffee and had to put the cup down before he dropped it. Judy was standing with her hands on her hips, filling the doorway, blocking out the light. She cast a cold shadow. Ted gathered himself for a storm.

But, Judy's reaction wasn't what Ted expected.

'I know what you've been doing,' she said. 'I only hope they've all gone to good homes.'

'Of course they have,' Ted lied. He didn't let on that Esmerelda had died a heroine, tied to a stake and shoved onto the community bonfire beside the Guy.

'We must come to an agreement, Ted. I don't want to lose them all. How many can . . .?'

'You can keep ten,' Ted said with all the conviction of a man who knows he's got his own way and can afford to sound benevolent.

'And they can still be my babies?'

'Yes.'

'And we can still have parties and picnics?'

'If you must.'

Then, Judy smiled a strange smile which didn't quite reach her eyes and said,

'You old Grizzly, you. You've always been my number one cuddles.'

***

So, there are ten little, furry dinner guests around the table this evening for Ted's sixtieth birthday. He's wearing his new dark blue birthday tie with little yellow Teddy bears all over it and is doing his best to go along with Judy's party. The wine is helping. The more of it he throws down his neck, the more it seems to be helping. He supposes there are worse things his wife might choose to do than sew Teddy bears and sell them for silly money.

He observes her pretending to fill Barnaby's cup. She takes a tissue and wipes the bear's mouth and her upper arm sags and jiggles as she rubs his furry snout. Ted downs the last of his fifth glass. He reaches out for the second bottle.

When he looks up again, the table and the candles are wobbling. He shakes his head and with the back of his hand wipes away beads of sweat from his top lip. The candles are melting into the table and so are the plates. The bears and Judy all seem to be dancing before his eyes. He tries to refocus and put things back where they belong. It's all getting mixed up.

Judy is wider than ever and when she stands up, she towers over him. She's laughing. But it's not *her* laugh. It's louder, deeper. Her large mouth is full of pointed, sharp teeth and, above it, her black nose has wide, cavernous nostrils.

'I don't feel very well,' he says.

Someone helps him into the bedroom and takes off his clothes. He knows he should reach for his pyjamas, but the light has gone out and he really needs to lie down. His head hurts. It's as if there's something inside it hammering to get out and there are terrible images battering his brain.

He tosses his head against the pillow, but the images grow clearer. He doesn't want these pictures in his head. He tries to concentrate on making them go away, but they won't budge.

Judy is massively pregnant. Her huge belly is wider than her backside. She doubles over in pain and tells him the babies are coming. He follows her to the bathroom where she squats and begins to thrust. He doesn't want to look. It's too horrible. Dear God, she's growling and she's reaching inside herself with her hairy hands. Jesus, she's pulling the creatures out of her. Two slimy bear cubs drop onto the bath mat. The sight of them makes him vomit. It comes up into his mouth and he spits it out.

***

Morning light pricks at his gluey eyelids. He tries to move his head but it's too heavy. His legs won't move either. Something is holding them down. There is a smell of sick. He stretches his face and his eyelashes part enough for him to make out little yellow figures sitting at the end of the bed, watching him. One in particular is like a ghost from the past. He remembers that exact same bear strapped to the back of the Henderson's Labrador.

'Buster? Is that you? I thought you were dead.'

Ted's voice sounds thick and muffled.

His hands won't move. He manages to move his head enough to look down at his body and he screams a stifled scream. He is covered in curly, yellow hair. He twists his neck as far as he is able. There are more little figures on Judy's dressing table. There sit Felicity, Eric, Esmerelda, Lucky and Clive, all with new clothes, new bodies and heads, ears and limbs.

The bedroom door opens and he can hear Judy's voice.

'Here we are,' she says. 'Here we all are. Isn't this lovely? Now we've got a real daddy, haven't we children?'

Ted tries to speak but she ignores his mumbled sounds.

'I suppose you're wondering what happened. Aren't you, Ted? Don't bother trying to answer. I can't hear what you're saying.'

She sits on the edge of the bed beside him. He can feel her weight on the mattress but hasn't got a clear view of her. 'You must think I'm an idiot,' she's saying. 'I told you before, Ted. You're the one who's the idiot. Not me. Lie still, sweetheart. It's no use struggling. You can't get up yet. I've had help to tie you down. Barbara has been helping me get everything ready for this for months. Barbara. Of course, you never bothered to use her name, did you? It's quite insulting, really, to be called Mrs Jim as if you haven't an identity of your own.

'Anyway, as I was saying, Barbara has been helping me and so has Theresa. Mrs Waddington to you, Ted. She had the sense to get rid of her husband years ago. Lie still. You'll listen to this, Ted, if it's the last thing you do.

'Theresa has a laptop and a mobile phone that takes pictures. She also has a car neither you nor Jim recognised when she followed the pair of you.'

Judy stands where Ted can see her. She's holding up Mrs Waddington's laptop so he can see the pictures on the screen: a mouldering mass of fabric and stuffing in his weed killer watering can; a trussed up body, hanging by ribbons, slashed to its core and its innards spilling; mutilated limbs poking out of a compost heap and a sweet little face sizzling and turning black as flames eat it away.

'You didn't really think I was going to let you get away with this, did you?' Judy says as she closes the laptop and puts it down. 'No, don't bother to answer. I was there on bonfire night. We all were. Theresa took us in her car. We saw what you did, you and Jim. You must be sick in the head, both of you.'

She releases the bungee straps holding Ted down on the bed. He lifts his arms to free himself but they end in huge paws and he can't do anything with them. An image of Judy sewing large pieces for her *commission* floats before his eyes.

'I did think about using Superglue,' Judy is saying, 'but in the end I decided that wouldn't be necessary. You are well and truly stitched up, Ted.'

Ted screams, but the sound is deadened and throbs in his ears. He raises his paws to his head but it's encased inside a new outer head. He struggles to sit up on the bed and looks at his reflection in the dressing table mirror. He is a life-sized Teddy with a hand-sewn snout.

'Judy,' he tries to say, 'stop this now.'

His words sound garbled behind the half mask. Only his eyes are free.

'You can't get out,' Judy says. 'I told you. I've sewn you in.'

Ted hunches his shoulders and twists his back.

She's sewn him in? Dear God.

He remembers once suspecting how Judy had the makings of a dangerous adversary, but he can't feel anything pulling at his skin. Surely, she's only sewn the ridiculous costume around him?

'The girls helped me,' Judy is saying. 'Well, you were completely out of it last night. How many had you had? 'Course, they all had a bit of added something just to make sure you wouldn't come round. Theresa's sleeping pills, as a matter of fact, all crunched up and sprinkled in the wine. So, after we'd sorted you out and strapped you on the bed, we went round to number eleven and did the same to Jim. Barbara will be with him now, talking to him, just like I'm talking to you. Theresa's taking the pictures again. Oh, I didn't show you the rest, did I? Here they are.'

She reaches for the laptop to show him what he looks like, naked, drugged, with the three women putting him in his Teddy bear's outfit.

'We could hardly do it for laughing,' Judy says. 'And, I should think they'll have a damned good laugh at the bowling club when they see this. Wouldn't you say so? Well of course you would if you could speak.'

On the laptop, there are similar images of Jim all trussed up and looking pathetic.

'What do you want me to do?' Ted says.

'Sorry, I can't hear you.'

'What do you want me to do?'

'I want you to make a choice, Ted,' she says. 'A bit like the one you gave me. *Me, or the bears,* you said. Well, I made my choice. Now it's your turn. You've seen the pictures of poor Clive and the others. Let's see, hanging, decapitation, stabbing, burning. Which way would *you* like to go?'

Ted rushes at her but she steps to the side and he falls over his large Teddy bear feet.

'It's your choice, Ted,' Judy says as he tries to right himself. 'I think that's more than fair. It's more choice than you gave my bears, after all. I mean, you wouldn't want to spend the rest of your life wearing that thing, would you? How would you eat? How would you go to the toilet? It would be a very messy end, sweetheart. Much better to end it quickly. The girls will help.'

She'd gone mad. Stark, raving mad, Ted thought as he sat on the floor. How on earth did these women think they could get away with it? Mad as hatters, the lot of them.

'Come on, Ted,' Judy says. 'We haven't got all day. You've got to stick to your plans when you've bodies to dispose of. 'Course, you'd know all about that, wouldn't you? Well, we thought you'd be dumbstruck, the girls and I. We're not stupid. We realised you wouldn't be able to make that choice. So we've made it for you. Theresa, are you ready?'

The door opens again, and there's Mrs Waddington, holding up a camera. From behind her, there's a shuffling and grunting noise and another life-size Teddy bear, this time in a frock and bonnet, follows her into the bedroom, pushed from behind by Mrs Jim.

'Get on the bed, Jim,' Judy says. 'Or should I say, Jemima? Here's your boyfriend, look, waiting for you. Ted, you get on there, too.'

Ted follows instructions; he doesn't know what else to do. He sits on the bed next to Jim. Their curly, yellow legs stick out in front of them like toys on a shelf. Ted can see their reflection in Judy's dressing table mirror.

Were these crazed women going to do them in right here in the bedroom and film it? Mrs Waddington comes closer with the camera. Judy and Mrs Jim arrange the men's paws so they look like they're holding hands.

'Right then, you two,' Judy says. 'This is how it's going to be. *This* is the only choice you get.'

Mrs Waddington zooms in. Ted can hear her camera. Judy continues.

'Henceforward, on the anniversary of this day,' she says, 'which just happens to be the day after your birthday, Ted, we will gather at twenty nine Laburnum Grove in memory of the victims of your violent rampage. In honour of said victims, even though they have been reborn, so to speak, and at this moment *bear* witness to this agreement, Ted and Jim will wear these costumes and sit at table without anything to eat while myself, Barbara and Theresa enjoy a champagne dinner.'

Blimey, Ted thinks, *she sounds like my mother and her mother all rolled into one.*

'Failure to comply will result in the immediate release of the films and pictures you have seen on Theresa's laptop and you will be the laughing stock not only on the Laburnums, but right across town and, in particular, at the bowling club. Happy Hour will never be the same again. You'd never live it down. We can go much further than that.Theresa knows how to put video films on the internet. The whole World Wide Web would know what you did and how we punished you. What do you say, gentlemen?'

Ted's stomach is like a lead weight. He is wondering how he and Jim might set about pilfering the Waddington woman's laptop, and getting them out of this mess but it seems Judy has that covered too.

'Don't even think about trying anything on,' she's saying. 'Have you heard of The Cloud, Ted? It's where you can store all your important documents in case your computer breaks down. Did you know you can even access, is that the right word, Theresa? You can *access* all your documents and *films* from your mobile phone. Isn't that amazing? Isn't that amazing, Ted? Ted?'

In the dressing table mirror Ted can see his and Jim's Teddy bear heads nodding in unison.

SP*ARSE* *from Merriam Webster Dictionary*
of few and scattered elements

DON AND YVONNE'S HOUSE OF SAINTS AND HERMITS

L'Ermitage des Oiseaux emerged from the steep hillside above Clermont as if it had grown out of it. In fact, Yvonne thought as she stepped, squinting, back outdoors into March sunlight, the basement spanning the full width of the property and accessible only from outside gave exactly that impression. Its rear wall was naked cliff face. Jutting stone ledges made for natural shelves and created dark niches for secret storage. The stones were dry and cool. There was a pleasant smell of clean earth and herbs. It was like a cave with an up and over door. Yvonne knew her husband would love it.

'Perfect. It's just what we've been looking for,' Don told the estate agent, who immediately snapped shut his clip file and agreed with vigorous nods and a six per cent commission-fuelled smile.

'Is it?' Yvonne said, the question ripe in her voice.

'Yes, of course, Madame,' the agent replied. 'There is much potential here.'

'Is there?' she said, taking in the rotting shutters and crumbling first floor balconies. A *little* renovation was what Don and she had agreed would be acceptable. She stepped back to get a better view of the roof. Ridge tiles had slipped and the chimney looked precarious. Property maintenance must not have been top priority for previous owners.

Rustic, moss-covered steps climbed to an enormous double door at centre front. Arched windows either side made the house look surprised. She turned to listen as the agent pointed out to Don the large plot with its boundaries that disappeared down the hill below them. At the far side of the plot, dilapidated outhouses fell over each other on the way down the slope and from the middle of tangled, giant euphorbia the remains of rusty kennel enclosures poked through like mantraps.

'And the view,' Don said, looking the other way, standing amid overgrown wild grasses, his hands on his hips as if he were already surveying his demesne. 'Just look at that view, Yvonne.'

'Ah, yes. The view, Monsieur. Incomparable,' the agent agreed with more nodding. 'You will never be, how you say, looked over.'

'Overlooked,' Don corrected. 'No, indeed. Not another house in sight. Parfait.' He breathed in deeply through his nose and let go the breath with an elongated '*Ahhh.*'

Yvonne grimaced. Don's *parfait* came out as *pairfay.* Twelve months' worth of French lessons hadn't helped in the pronunciation department. His vowel sounds were worst of all, but he thought he was much improved. When they went out, he ordered drinks with great aplomb, chose from menus with all the assurance of an ex-pat of many years' standing, and if shop assistants didn't understand what he was asking for, it was always their fault, not his. He was determined to enjoy *la vie Francaise,* and he was going to do it the way *he* wanted. Yvonne knew this surprised-looking house on a hill with its man cave for a basement was going to be *the* one for Don. This one had all the potential *he* was looking for. She hoped to find reasons of her own to fall in love with it herself.

'Was it a hermitage?' Yvonne asked the estate agent, thinking of all the other properties they'd seen in the last year, ones she'd had a soft spot for but Donald had rejected.

'Yes, Madame. In ancient times. Then, it was a simple house of one storey. The sainted gentleman who lived here had a special rapport with animals, so they say. Birds flocked to him. He made his simple home a lodging for travellers in these lonely hills. Of course, since then the house has been altered many times.'

'Sainted? He was a saint?'

'The people of the time treated him like one, Madame.'

'What was his name?'

'Nobody knew. He was simply *L'Ermite,* the Hermit.'

Things were looking up. The house had history. Yvonne liked that. It would be something to tell visitors.

Don banged on about L'Ermitage des Oiseaux relentlessly for the next forty eight hours. Their agreement had always been not to rush into anything. Things needed mulling over, especially with a project as big as this one was likely to be. But Don was smitten, bowled over by the size of the property and the great chunk of hillside included in the sale. Yvonne relented as she'd known from the first.

They signed the *compromis de vente,* paid the deposit and gave notice on their short-term rented apartment in town. For the next ten days, the mandatory cooling-off period, Don gushed about the beauties of the basement; how it would make perfect garaging for his four by four and her old, Citroën runabout; how there'd be bags of storage for outdoor furniture through winter; how he would finally have enough space for all his projects.

'What about those dangerous balconies?' Yvonne reminded him.

'Soon get those fixed,' he assured her. 'I'll get the boys in. We'll make short work of that. No problem.'

Yvonne passed no comment. At fifty-six and overweight, Don was the youngest *boy*. She couldn't imagine which one of them would be steady enough for the necessary ladder work. But, this was their new project now. L'Ermitage des Oiseaux was going to be their new home. Better to look on the bright side. It might turn out to be the best move they'd ever made.

Don and Yvonne Cooper moved their things up the winding track to their new home on a clear spring day with wild thyme-scented breezes riffling through the heath.

'*Pairfay*,' Don said in a contented way as he negotiated hairpin bends through stands of chestnuts and *Cypres de Provence* which Yvonne called pencil trees, dark and slim, like exclamation marks dotted about the hillsides. The track climbed further. Pine trees thinned and gave way to open scrub.

'Look at that view, Yvonne. Brilliant!'

Far below them the river Hérault twisted through deep gorges, cutting towns and villages in half as it rolled toward the sea. Yvonne peered backwards at the way they'd come. A snake of a road wound itself around the hills, clinging tight to rock faces, curling and bending and dropping into the far distance. She wondered how she'd cope with the dirt track through winter frosts. They probably even got snow this high.

Don turned into the gravel drive and pulled on the handbrake.

'Airmitarge day Wazoh,' he said, putting equal emphasis on every syllable. 'I wonder what kind of birds?'

'Vultures?' Yvonne suggested.

'No. You're being silly. Magnificent red kites. Eagles, maybe. I'll need some binoculars. Oh, yes. Lots to look forward to. Come on, old girl. Let's get stuck in.'

They struggled with the antiquated key and huge lock on the double doors, made of metal and heavy to move. Don put his shoulder to them and Yvonne pushed him from behind. Paint from the door peeled away on their hands and clothing to reveal extensive rusting beneath. The doors gave way with a metallic creak. Yvonne brushed away flakes of lilac paint from her well-worn shirt. She pulled back her hair and tightened the band holding it out of her eyes. She must find a hairdresser soon, she thought, before the state of it was past redemption. As the doors gave way, Don tripped on something on the floor. He stumbled across the vestibule. Yvonne almost fell on top of him.

'What the . . .?' he grumbled.

'It's for us, Don,' Yvonne said, straightening up and picking up the large manila envelope.

'What is it? Who is it from?'

'Well, if you just give me a minute to open it, I'll tell you.'

She tore open the package and slid out a colourful calendar: a gift from the estate agency. Each day displayed its saint's name with a bit of added information about the particular saint.

'It's only a calendar,' Don said. 'Nothing special. I bet they give them to everybody.'

'Look,' Yvonne said. 'There's a message in English: *we are wishing you a happy new home.* Oh, isn't that sweet?'

She stroked the glossy paper of the calendar as if it was a dear possession. Don paid no attention: he was off, into the house, taking possession like Lord of the Things. Yvonne wandered through the hall toward the kitchen area, looking for somewhere to hang the calendar. It felt like the right thing to do, treat this first house gift as something special, set the tone, so to speak, but the house was too dark to see where she was going.

'Stay where you are,' Don's voice came from out of the gloom. 'All the shutters are closed. I'll go round and open up all the rooms before we bring our things in.'

'I'll make us a cup of tea first,' Yvonne shouted back. 'When I can see what I'm doing.'

She stood in the dark, holding onto the calendar. She could hear Don moving about the house, the creak of metal locking-rods and subsequent groan of parched wooden shutters. Indoors, the house had a musty smell. Yvonne couldn't wait to throw open all the windows and let in some fresh air. The sounds of her husband taking possession of their new home grew more distant as he moved through the rooms. Then his footsteps came closer again, tapping against the tiled floors. A door opened and there he was, grinning like a big kid. He opened the kitchen shutters. Light flooded in.

'Where's that cup of tea, Missus?' he said.

'Coming right up,' she said. 'Is the power on?'

'Ah. Just a minute.'

He disappeared again and she heard him going outside. There was the noise of the basement door creaking open. She was still holding the calendar. She looked about for somewhere to put it. Below her, the basement door squeaked closed again. Don's footsteps came back up the front steps into the house. Still the power was off.

'It must be up here,' Don said as he came into the kitchen.

'What must?'

'The electricity control box.'

He went through the kitchen, opening cupboards. Behind a floor to ceiling door, he found the control box and flicked the switches. Lights flickered on the oven. Don went to fetch the kettle from the car.

Yvonne hung the calendar on a nail sticking out from the rear kitchen wall. It would serve as a reminder to pull the nail out. That nail could rip someone's eye out.

The calendar was forgotten once the removal van arrived with their furniture. The rest of the day flew by in a haze of shifting cartons and boxes, drinking hurried cups of tea, grabbing a slice of bread or a tomato to ward off hunger pangs. By dusk, the house was a tumbled mess, but all Yvonne wanted to do was sleep. Her hair felt dry and ratty and her feet ached.

'But I'm starving,' Don said.

'I'm done in, Donald. Can't do another thing.'

'Couldn't you just heat something up in the oven?'

'It isn't working. And there's no manual. The lights are flashing but the oven won't turn on.'

'Let me have a look at it.'

'Don, if you're hungry, go get a takeaway. We'll sort out the oven tomorrow.'

'What? Go all the way back down into town?'

'It'll be quickest.'

When he'd gone, Yvonne made up the bed. She would have had a shower if there'd been enough hot water, but the immersion heater didn't seem to be working properly either. She filled the kettle and waited for it to boil. She glanced at the calendar and started laughing at the date.

March 22nd Ste Léa:

Saint Léa renounced painting her face and adorning her head with shining pearls. She exchanged her rich attire for sackcloth. She dwelt in a corner with a few bits of furniture . . .

As Yvonne poured hot water into the bathroom sink and caught sight of herself in the mirror, she laughed again. Sackcloth? Living in a corner with a few sticks of furniture? She thought the *sainted gentleman* who'd once lived here would be amused at the coincidence of Don and Yvonne Cooper moving into his hermitage on the day of Saint Léa.

***

Three days later, on Sunday morning, as was usual, Yvonne called their daughter, Caroline. Don was in his basement.

'I'm on my mobile,' Yvonne said. 'We haven't got the phone connected yet, so I'll have to be quick.'

'So how is it going, Mum?' Caroline asked. 'How's Dad? Is it everything he dreamed of? We can't wait to come and visit.'

'Your father's in seventh heaven, planning this and that. He says he hasn't even got time to get a haircut. There's a lot of work to do. Most of it seems to be in the basement just now.'

'We'll all bring paintbrushes to help.'

'Structural work, Caroline. I wouldn't want you to bring the little ones yet, dear. My heart would be in my mouth the whole time.'

'A house with Romeo and Juliet balconies? It sounds fantastic.'

'Yes, but, they're very precarious.'

'Dad knows what he's doing, Mum. Don't worry.'

'And there's a heap of old junk to clear before we can make a garden. And we need a retaining wall and . . .'

'Mum, stop worrying. Everything will be fine. What's the matter with you?'

Yvonne sighed.

'I suppose I'm feeling a bit frustrated, Caroline,' she said. 'I can't get on with anything until your dad's done his bit. And neither of us is getting any younger.'

'That's what you said last time. Listen, Mum. Dad will do the place up as he always does and then you'll start looking for the next one. The only difference is, this time you're in France.'

'You know what, Caroline? I'm beginning to think I've had enough of renovation projects. Sometimes I think I'd like to live in comfort in my old age.'

'Mother! You're not old. Far from it.'

Yvonne thought it was a good thing her daughter couldn't see her in her ancient, plaster-splattered clothes and with her hair, grey at the roots and turning greyer by the day. She hurried through her chores in town, at the supermarkets and on market days and she tried not to notice other women, smartly turned out, with their hair neatly coiffed and with smart shoes on their pedicured feet. She couldn't remember the last time she'd worn a pair of shoes with heels.

'Why don't you keep a diary?' Caroline suggested. 'You know, day-by-day work in progress. Then, when you've got your computer going, I'll help you make a blog with before and after pictures.'

It sounded like a reasonable idea.

'Well, I suppose it would help take my mind off things,' Yvonne agreed.

On the first Wednesday in April, Don drove them to the market in Clermont. Hordes of Easter visitors, pushing prams and pulling dogs, packed the narrow passages between stalls. The tourists stopped to buy their *pains au chocolat* and caused bottlenecks in the pack. They stopped again to take photos of colourful fruit and vegetable displays, strings of garlic, baskets of fresh mussels and oysters from the étang down near the coast and more photos of their children eating the pains au chocolat.

Don and Yvonne bought cheeses and charcuterie from the sausage man. They had to forego *café crème* at their favourite bar. All the tables were taken. They pressed on through noisy crowds. In a jumble of half-price knick-knacks and plastic bits and pieces, Yvonne found what she was looking for. She bought a page-a-day diary and put it in a new washing up bowl with a pack of pegs and a washing line and on the way back home, she didn't look at the scenery or worry about hairpin bends.

'You're quiet,' Don said, shifting down into second.

'I was thinking.'

'What about?'

'I don't know what to put in a diary. I've never kept one before.'

'What did Caroline suggest?'

'Day by day progress on the house.'

'Well, there you are then.'

That evening, alone in their bedroom while Don was still messing about under the house, Yvonne picked up her pen.

Wednesday April 4th

Don spends a lot of time in the basement. Sometimes I wonder what he's doing in there. He never has anything to show for it.

Thursday April 5th

Don left early for the Brico. He says you have to be there for opening time or else the special offers on DIY get snapped up. He wouldn't say what he was going to buy. I went outside, intending to look in the basement to see what's going on. I couldn't get in. Don had closed the door and it wouldn't budge.

Friday April 6th

Don showed me the new remote control system he's going to fit for opening the up and over door to the basement.

By Saturday, Yvonne couldn't think of anything else to write in her diary. There was little progress to report. Don spent the whole day in his basement, surfacing only for refreshment.

'Most of the boys and their wives are away in England for the Easter break,' Yvonne told Caroline during another hasty, Sunday mobile call.

'Haven't you got your phone in yet?' Caroline said.

'Caroline, this is France.'

'Book a flight and come to us for a while, Mum.'

'I couldn't leave him here on his own.'

'Why not? He'd be in his element, pottering about, doing his own thing.'

'Exactly. That's exactly what I mean. I don't want him *pottering*. I need him to get on with repairs to this house.'

After a brief catch up with her grandchildren about what they were doing at school, Yvonne closed the call. She could hear Don scratching away at something or other in the basement. She stepped outside, down the front steps and found him, in the open up and over doorway, fiddling with a bicycle.

'Where did you get that from?' she said.

'Emmaüs. They do house clearances. Big Bill told me about it. It's like an Aladdin's cave in that place.'

Yvonne wondered what it was about caves, basements and sheds that men found so attractive, but she tried to look interested and said,

'What do you want a bike for?'

'What do you think I want a bike for? I'm going to ride it. Cycle to the village to fetch bread.'

'Donald, which village would that be?'

'I'll find one. All these tracks up here are bound to lead somewhere.'

There was little to be gained from pointing out that the return climb would be beyond him. She left him tinkering and went indoors to find something to do. She would have to be patient with him. He was enjoying himself playing in his man cave. Just a little more patience. All the *boys* were away. Major construction work couldn't start without a team of helpers. House repairs would happen eventually. Just a little more patience.

She got on with some baking. Using the Pyro-Technique oven she'd inherited from previous owners of the hermitage required vigilance. Designed with a programme to self-clean by burning off spills, it would have been the height of luxury when it was new. She and Don had worked out how to make the thing start by resetting the clock, but the thermostat was broken. After twenty minutes, it reached incinerator heat and Yvonne had to take out whatever was baking, whether or not it was properly cooked. Simple pastry dishes worked okay. Twenty minutes was all they needed, as long as the filling was pre-cooked. Anything more exotic was out of the question. Before she went to bed that night, she scribbled a little note in the diary.

Sunday 8th April
I'll just have to use the hob.

L'Ermitage des Oiseaux
Saturday May 5th

Today is the day of Saint Judith. It says so on my calendar. Every day is a Saint's day, apparently. Saint Judith said the way to God was through painful physical suffering, exile in a foreign land and being poor by choice.

Don is suffering. Every muscle in his body aches from pretending he's good enough to enter the Tour de France. The push bike has been relegated to the back of the cave. I am also suffering. I burned my arm on the Pyro-Technique, giving it another chance. We will have more cold food in future.

We ***are*** *exiled in a foreign land.*

If ever we get this house finished, we will be extremely poor.

It has been an exasperating month.

It was lovely to have a proper length conversation on the landline with Caroline next day.

'How's Dad?'

'He's growing his hair.'

'What?'

'Yes. He's going all *Frenchified.* He says he wants it in a pony tail.'

'Mother! You can't let him do that. He'll look ridiculous.'

'I know, dear, but he's got his heart set on it. You know what he's like when he sets his mind. And he's bought a hat.'

'What kind of a hat?'

'A black, felt one with a wide brim. He says it'll look good when his pony tail is long enough.'

'Mother!'

On May 10th, the day of Saint Solange, who according to Yvonne's calendar protected communities from drought, Don's friend, Big Bill, a diminutive Scotsman, arrived to do something about the dangerous Romeo and Juliet balconies. Rain came down in torrents. They spent most of their time discovering new leaks where driving wind forced the deluge under the roof tiles to splash into rooms below. They ran out of buckets and bowls and had to use Yvonne's saucepans to catch the drips. A symphony of plops and drizzles rang through the house.

'What can we do about the balconies?' Yvonne wanted to know.

'Not much in this weather,' Don said. 'Don't worry, we'll think of something.'

Don and Big Bill disappeared into the basement after a lunch of Yvonne's leek and potato soup warmed up on the hob. She could hear the men hammering and sawing beneath the house. A smell of burning metal rose from below. Rain still lashed the house. She switched on the radio to drown the violent screeches from the basement. They were giving her earache. She kept out of the way when Don and Big Bill came indoors, dripping more water over her floors. Later, she went upstairs to view the results of their handiwork.

Waist high corrugated metal sheets, like barricades, spanned the width of the French windows in all the bedrooms. Yvonne's face fell.

'It's only a temporary fix,' Don said. 'To stop anybody stepping outside.'

‘Temporary is fine,’ Big Bill said with a shrug. ‘It’s the French way. They choose their friends because of who they are, not for what they’ve got. They don’t care if your garden wall isn’t finished or your shutters aren’t painted.’

After a slice of burnt chocolate cake, Big Bill took his leave. Rain still fell like javelins, thudding against the up and over door to the basement, lashing at the house, cascading down the front steps.

‘It comes in threes,’ Big Bill said as he got into his battered Peugeot. ‘If it goes into a fourth day, you can be sure you’ll get six.’

L’Ermitage des Oiseaux
Saturday May 19th

Today is the day of Saint Yves who is the patron saint of lawyers and attorneys.

The rain has finally stopped after six days of downpours and another three grey and drizzly. Hopefully, Don will have the roofers in before it happens again.

He made a big show of inviting me to view his man cave today. I had to wait outside while he performed a ceremony with his new remote control.

‘State of the art,’ *he called his new locking system. He’s fitted automated side and vertical deadbolts, whatever they are. He sang a little fanfare and waved the remote about like a magic wand from Ollivanders. Then the up and over door opened up to reveal . . .*

. . . a cosy den. A DEN in his man cave. It’s complete with a winged armchair he’s picked up from some junk shop on one of his forays. He stood there, grinning, when he showed me it. I couldn’t believe what he’s done. All this time I’ve been waiting for him to fix the cooker, sort the roof out, any number of other, smaller jobs he could have been getting on with, but no. He’s been spending all his time down there in that blasted basement, fixing it up like a bachelor pad. He’s made sets of shelves and an L-shaped workbench across one side. It’s better fitted than my kitchen. He’s

even got a drinks cabinet and a bottled gas heater. No wonder he didn't want me going down there nosing around. We'll never get the cars in now. I've no idea why he needs such lock-up security.

Nobody else lives up here but us.

The bill arrived today from the Notary.

***

The day the cat appeared, Yvonne's patience was pushed to the limit. She'd gone down to the basement to take Don a cup of coffee and found him, sitting in his armchair, stroking a mangled mess of fur wrapping itself around his ankles. It was the mangiest looking creature she'd ever seen. Yvonne wanted rid of it.

'But it's very clean,' Don said.

'Probably all that rain,' Yvonne said. 'I don't want it anywhere near the house, Don. I've enough mess to clean up indoors. The mattress is still damp, the furniture's got patches on where the rain came in and . . .'

'Poor thing,' Don said and reached out to pick up the feline intruder.

'Don, I'd be careful if I were you.'

The cat hissed at her.

'She's hungry,' Don said.

'It's wild. Just look at it. That cat is feral.'

'How do you know?'

'Because nobody but us lives up here, Don.'

L'Ermitage des Oiseaux

Wednesday May 23rd

Saint Didier liked strict discipline, apparently.

Don says the cat will keep his basement free from vermin. We bought cat food at the market today. I don't know why he's taken to it. It won't let me anywhere near it. It just shows up and makes the nastiest howling noise when it wants food. It's got eyes in the back of its head, too, and can tell if I come too close, even while it's bent over its dish. It looks as if it's ready to pounce all the time. And it does. Whenever I walk past. It'll get the toe of my shoe up its backside if it does it again.

Don has given it a name. Didier, like on the calendar. Didi for short.

Caroline and her family went away for the English Spring Bank holiday. Yvonne was missing them and wished she'd taken up their offer of sharing a week in a Cornish cottage.

'You can go with them next time,' Don suggested. 'Anyway, why would you want to be in Cornwall when you've got all this?'

He held out his arms and swept them in an arc over the panoramic view in front of the house. 'Skies so blue, it hurts your eyes; wild flowers . . .'

'Wild cats,' Yvonne said, regarding the troupe of eight that Didi had brought from under the disused kennels. 'But no birds. No birds anywhere. The cats have probably eaten them all.'

'You're just being silly,' Don said and smiled at his furry friends.

'Don, I'm not being silly. I'm being fed up. Fed up to the back teeth, Donald. Are you listening? When are you going to start on the house? I can hardly see what I'm doing in the kitchen since the light fitting broke. That bloody kitchen'll be the death of me, Don. Not to mention that bloody useless oven.'

Don gave a Gallic shrug so pronounced that his pony tail flipped upwards and nearly knocked off his black Boston felt.

'There's no rush,' he said. 'We're in France. Nobody rushes. It happens when it happens. Relaxez-vous.'

He turned away from his wife and disappeared into the basement. Didi and her troupe followed.

L'Ermitage des Oiseaux
Saturday June 2nd
Today is the day of Saint Blandine. The Romans put her to torture by animals.

Don slipped on some of Didi's doo-doo and fell on top of the cat. I've never heard such howling. The cat squawked as well and shot up the steps into the house. Don hobbled after it while I cleaned up the mess smeared on the steps. The next thing I knew, there was a great rumbling noise followed by an almighty crash and clouds of dust. The cat came flying back outside, launched itself down the hill and disappeared. When I looked back at the house and the dust cleared, there was a pile of rubble on the grass. One of the Romeo and Juliet balconies lay in pieces. Don lay in a crumpled heap beside the broken stones. He was very quiet. I called an ambulance.

He has a broken hip. Fortunately, we're still covered by our E106 so we'll be reimbursed the cost of his treatment. I've decided not to call Caroline on her mobile. I don't want to spoil their holiday.

Yvonne was too busy over the next few weeks to pay attention to her diary or the saints' days on the calendar. The round trip to the clinic to visit Don took up the best part of the day, not least because of the time it took her to negotiate the hairpin bends on the track from and to the house. She hardly dare take her foot from the brake downhill. The way down was on the outside edge with sheer drops and not much in the way of protective barriers. On the way up, her old Citroën struggled to make it, choking and spluttering in second gear.

She took Don fruit and the fizzy drinks and chocolate he requested. He said the hospital food was quite good, but he missed his regular little treats. Yvonne's own meals consisted of cold cuts and sandwiches. She couldn't be bothered to battle with the oven.

Don never asked how she was getting on alone. He was more worried about the cats.

'You won't forget to feed them, will you?' he said. 'I know you don't like them, Yvonne, but it's not like you to be cruel to animals.'

After his hip replacement. Don was put on a diet. The doctors had been so thorough, they'd uncovered a problem neither he nor Yvonne knew anything about. High cholesterol. It came as a bit of a shock to Don when Yvonne stopped taking in his sugary drinks and chocolate.

'You're not allowed them now,' she said. 'It's for your own good.'

During the time Don was in hospital, Yvonne did her best to see to the troupe of cats. She fed them twice a day and cleaned up the messes they made in Don's basement. All nine of them watched her with disdain, their green eyes almost luminous in the half-shade. If she was late with their evening biscuits, they formed a circle round her and stared, and when they had deigned to eat, they turned their backs on her and with supercilious strides went off to make another mess.

On Saint Alban's Day, Friday 22nd June, Don came home.

'Haven't you noticed,' Yvonne said, 'how the saints' days on the calendar seem to coincide with what we're doing?'

'Not really,' he said, lowering himself into his winged armchair.

'Don't you want to come inside?'

'I'm more comfortable in this chair,' he said. 'The sofa is too low.'

'Why didn't you say? I'll carry your chair inside for you.'

'I'd rather stay here,' he said. 'I've got shade and with the door open I can still see the view. But, I'd like a cup of tea.'

She bit back on her frustration and went into the house. In her kitchen, the oven still burned everything. The light fitting was still broken. The calendar still hung on a protruding nail that she couldn't remove.

Saint Alban, she thought. *The first English martyr. Oh, I want to go home.*

She took a throw from the sitting room, made Don his tea and a ham sandwich. When she went back to the basement, he was asleep in his armchair. She covered him with the soft throw and took away the tea.

Don slept on the sofa that night. He couldn't manage any more stairs, he said, after the ones to get inside the house. Alone again in their bedroom, Yvonne opened the French windows. The night was warm; the sky full of stars. She stood by the corrugated barricade and let the warm air blow against her bare arms. She rubbed at the pain in her ear and took another two anti-inflammatory pills.

It could be wonderful here, she thought. *But it isn't.*

Don improved over the next few days. He was able to move around more easily and there was less pain, he said. He cleared a path from the bottom of the front steps to his basement so he wouldn't trip on anything hidden in the long grass. He started a bit of maintenance on both cars.

From underneath the washing line, dodging stray rocks and avoiding tussocks, Yvonne watched him work as she hung out bed linen. The breeze aggravated the pain in her ear. Most likely she'd picked up an infection from somewhere, she thought. If it didn't put itself right soon, she'd have to see a doctor.

L'Ermitage des Oiseaux
Sunday June 24th.
St John Baptiste

Saint John the Baptist lived as a hermit and preached that the kingdom of heaven was close at hand. I don't like to think about how he ended.

Caroline wants me to come. She says Don is being unreasonable and it would do him good to manage on his own for a while. I reminded her about his recent operation, but she pointed out how he'd been able to do all the things he wanted to. I could hardly hear what she was saying. My ear seems to be blocked and now the other one has started. It might be better to go see the doctor in England.

Don spends more time than ever in the basement. He's made the cats some sleeping platforms. They curl up like soft toys on toy shop shelves and let their tails hang over the edge. And, to tell the truth, Don's stupid pony tail would look better on a cat!

Monday June 25th.
Saint Prosper of Aquitaine

He believed in the doctrines of grace and predestination and the gift of perseverance.
I am trying to maintain the good grace to persevere.

Tuesday June 26th
Saint Anthelme
He restored and improved the buildings at Grande Chartreuse, including constructing a defensive wall and an aqueduct.

Our 'neufbox' was delivered today, so now I've got the computer up and running. Don has run a water supply to the basement. He says it'll be handy to hose the garden. What garden?
I had a quick look on Ryanair. There's a new route from Béziers to Manchester. Caroline could pick me up. My earache is a little better but my hearing is still affected.

Yvonne called all the *boys* to try and muster some support and maybe get a few jobs finished around the house. She had to ask people to shout down the phone so she could hear what they were saying. Big Bill had gone to Disney with the grandkids. The others were planning trips away or had visitors staying with them and had no free time.

L'Ermitage des Oiseaux
Tuesday July 3rd
Saint Thomas is the patron saint of architects. I thought he was the one who doubted Christ had risen.

Well, I doubt Don is ever going to rise off his fat backside and make a proper start on this house. He sits in that flaming armchair of his talking to the cats and making himself cups of tea on the camp stove. What was the point of taking on this property if he'd no intentions of ever doing anything with it? The bloody basement is all he's interested in. That, and the cats.

He's moved a single bed in there, too. I'm not bothered about that; I've got used to sleeping on my own. But I refuse to serve him his meals in that sodding man cave. He can bloody well shift his fat arse.

Friday July 13th
Saint Henry is the patron saint of the childless, the handicapped and those rejected by Religious Order.

Don says he enjoys sleeping in the basement with the cats. He says it's cooler in there. He's never once asked me how I am. He must know my ears are still a problem but he doesn't seem to care.

I miss my family. People who care about me.

I've booked a flight. I'll tell Don tomorrow.

Next day, it was evening before Yvonne told Don she was going to England. He'd annoyed her all day, him and his basement and his cats and she knew she couldn't talk to him until her anger had dissipated. As much as she felt frustrated and disappointed about his lack of interest in their home, she didn't want their last proper conversation to be a row. She kept out of his way and he didn't seem to notice that they'd shared hardly a word over lunch. When he'd eaten, he went straight back to the basement.

Yvonne gave her husband the news she was going away for a few weeks after they'd had dinner and she was making coffee. He was hanging around waiting for his cup. The cats were hanging around waiting on the front steps.

Don shrugged and said,

'If that's what you want to do.'

'Pardon?' she said.

'I said okay, if that's what you want to do.'

'Don't you want to know when I'm going?'

'Does it matter?' he said.

'Pardon?'

'I'll know, won't I, when you're not here? I'll have my girls to keep me company. What's the matter with your ears? You keep rubbing them.'

He didn't wait for her answer. He took his coffee and drifted back to the basement and the nine cats followed him.

Yvonne stormed to their room. Angry and hot, she set about planning her packing. Mad thoughts of leaving for England and never coming back raced through her mind as she pulled things from drawers and laid them out on her bed.

He was calling the cats *his girls* now. What had got into him? Hadn't she shown patience enough? Hadn't she tried to have the good grace to persevere? Those saints on her calendar hadn't had Don to put up with.

She was aware of movement outside her window. She went to stand by the ugly metal barricade and watched fireworks lighting up the night sky. Of course, July 14th, Bastille Day. She knew there would be music and celebrations in the valley below. She couldn't hear it and she couldn't hear the whizz-bangs of the sky rockets as they pierced the night, but she watched from her bedroom window as they unzipped the darkness and burst into huge circles of brilliant stars.

Something flashed past her legs. She looked down to see Didi, scurrying around the room, its eyes wild, its fur sticking up all over. The cat leapt onto her bed and got its claws stuck in the fabric of Yvonne's best summer skirt.

'Get out!' she yelled at the cat. She batted it with a sandal.

The cat launched itself from the bed, yowling and dragging Yvonne's skirt behind it. Didi raced madly round the room. Yvonne's skirt caught on a splinter at the corner of the wardrobe. Yvonne watched, in horror, as her best skirt split into two. The cat was free now and it lunged for the door, flying down the stairs and out the door. From the window, Yvonne could see it heading for the basement. She bent down to retrieve her ruined outfit and didn't see how the cat, leaping through long grass, stepped on the remote control lying in front of the basement where Don had left it. She didn't see how the up and over door closed itself. She didn't hear the deadbolts clunk into place. She didn't know Don was asleep inside, unaware of what was happening.

***

Next morning, Yvonne had an early start for check-in at the airport. Don hadn't offered to take her. In fact, Don hadn't even bothered to come out of his cave to say goodbye. Yvonne shouted through the locked up and over door.

'I'm going now. Donald. Don't be silly. I'm going now.'

There was no response. One of the cats skittered past her. It had a dead creature in its maw: a rat-looking thing, but fatter. Yvonne shuddered. There'd be innards and other horrors to clean up somewhere soon. Well, it would be up to Don to clean up the cats' messes for a month or so.

She went back inside the house for a last check she hadn't forgotten anything. The calendar flapped in the breeze from the open door.

July 15th Saint Donald of Ogilvy

Saint Donald of Ogilvy founded a religious order with his nine daughters.

The irony was not lost on Yvonne as she imagined Don, hiding in his man cave with his nine *girls.* He was welcome to them.

Stupid bloody caveman, she thought as she climbed into her Citroën.

***

Sitting in silence in his winged armchair, Don heard a car door slam. He was in a confused fog of anger and resentment. Why hadn't Yvonne answered his call for help? He'd been shouting and banging on the up and over door for hours last night. He'd had to pee in a bucket before getting into his single bed. He'd struggled in the dense darkness inside his cave to find the light switch.

Two could play at that game. He could stay in his cave for as long as he liked. He'd be fine; he had water and the gas ring. He'd manage. He had all his tools. He had power. He could cut his way out when he was ready. It ought not take long. Then, he and his girls would have the whole place to themselves. He got up and boiled his kettle.

He heard the old diesel engine start up: Yvonne's Citroën. He settled in his armchair, contented with his coffee. The engine noise stopped. Don heard footsteps going into the house. He raised his cup to his mouth but he lost sight of it. Everything went black. His overhead light and the lamp by his armchair had gone off. He reached for the lamp switch but, in the darkness, knocked it from the table. He heard the light bulb smash on the concrete floor. He couldn't see a thing. Not a crack of daylight penetrated his security system.

The footsteps came back to stop outside.

'I know you can hear me, you old fool,' Yvonne shouted. 'I've switched the electricity off. Now you'll have to come out of there.'

His stomach sank. His senses froze. In solid blackness, he felt his way around the side of the basement to the up and over door and hit it with balled fists.

'Yvonne,' he shouted. 'I can't get out.'

'Donald,' Yvonne shouted. 'I've had enough of your silly games. I'm going to Caroline's. I'll give you a call when I feel up to it.'

***

At her feet, the cat that had had the rat-looking creature was watching her with sly, green eyes. Its back was hunched and what appeared to be slimy intestines were hanging from its mouth. Something grey was oozing from them. Yvonne turned away.

***

Donald heard the car engine start again. Cold fear froze him. How was he going to escape? Without light, without power, how was he going to find a way out? And even if he did figure out a way to beat the deadlocks, how would he survive in the meantime? How long would he be able to last? He had water on tap, but what about food? His secret stash of chocolate stuffed into a gap between rocks in the rear wall wouldn't last long.

And then it hit him. The car. Her old Citroën. He'd never completed the maintenance on it. He hadn't replaced the brake fluid. He had to stop her. She'd never make it round the first hairpin.

'Yvonne!' he yelled, but the car pulled away.

Donald Cooper of L'Ermitage des Oiseaux found his way back to his armchair and sat. He could hear scratching at the door and knew his girls were trying to reach him. His thoughts wandered.

How long would it be before someone noticed a car that had gone over the edge? From the documents in the glove compartment, they'd be able to trace the Citroën to this address. And the body inside it. They would come to the house and they would hear him shouting for help. Would he be able to survive on rations till then?

Yvonne's death wouldn't be his fault. He didn't know she was planning to go to England till last night. If he'd known she was going to use the car soon, he would have fixed the brakes properly. No, it couldn't be his fault. And anyway, she'd locked him in the basement. Everyone would be able to see he hadn't been in a position to stop her. He sat, listening to the cats scratching and prepared himself for the wait.

***

Yvonne settled into the back seat of the taxi she'd called at the last minute and said to the driver,

'Béziers airport, please.'

It made more sense to use the taxi service rather than leave her old car at the airport, especially as she wasn't quite sure when she'd be coming back.

***

In the overgrown garden at L'Ermitage des Oiseaux, nine cats were digging to make a tunnel under the up and over door. All of them had gifts for their sainted master. Some of the gifts were still alive.

ENHE*ARSE from the website lexic.us*
referring to the opportunity or privilege of being heard

MY TURN TO SPEAK

My turn to speak is coming up. Nerves pummel my stomach and my mouth feels dry.

I know they'll be kind. They will empathise with my situation. They'll give their support. I can imagine their gentle eyes, their crooked little smiles, heads tilted in sympathy or nodding in agreement. They'll encourage me. At first.

Joyce invites me to stand. I fix my gaze on the wall clock at the back of the room so I don't have to make direct eye contact.

'I don't know where to begin,' I say to the group.

Joyce uncrosses her legs and lays her arms across the clipboard on her lap.

'Tell us why you're here,' she suggests.

My ears feel hot. I hope the redness doesn't spread to my face. I take a deep breath. Stare at the clock.

'I'm not assertive enough,' I say.

Joyce leans towards me.

'Good,' she says. 'Now turn that thought into a positive statement.'

I know what she means but my head is empty. I can't think of the words. I remember what some of the others have said before me.

'I want to be more assertive.'

Applause goes around the semicircle of women. My eyes slip from the clock and I catch sight of the heads and smiles, just as I had imagined. I've started now; I may as well continue.

'I can't stand it any more,' I tell them.

They wait. They smile some more.'But, I don't know how to stop it.'

A bell rings in the corridor outside the school classroom we use for our afternoon sessions. We can hear chairs scraping the floor, doors slamming. A swarm of navy blue uniforms buzzes past our window. Heels clack on hard floors. Voices rise through the octaves as the corridor fills.

'Thank you, Helen,' Joyce says to me. 'Will you begin for us next time?'

I have to go home now and I don't want to. I put up my umbrella against February sleet and hurry across the school forecourt, hoping none of the others will want to stop and talk. I'd like to linger but I really have to go home now and face what's waiting.

John hovers while I'm cooking dinner. He always does. He looks over my shoulder to check on what I'm making.

'Ah, chilli,' he says. 'One of my favourites.'

He doesn't move away. He inspects what I'm doing and looks at his watch. I know what he's going to say next and it makes me grit my teeth.

'What time will it be ready?' he asks.

He always asks. Every day. It's one of his habits. As soon as he comes home, it's the first thing he does. Comes to the kitchen to supervise and ask what time dinner will be ready.

'In about an hour,' I tell him.

He looks at his watch again.

'That's six minutes later than usual,' he says.

'I know, John. I've been out this afternoon.'

'Why?'

I want to shout at him. I want to say I've every right to go out on my day off work.

'I went to meet some friends,' I say instead.

'You've put only one teaspoon of chilli paste in, Helen. You usually put two.'

I want to tell him to go away and leave me alone. No, that's not true. I want to tell him to piss off and leave me alone.

'Thank you,' I say.

Fifty five minutes later he begins his getting- ready- for- dinner routine. He checks through glasses in the wall cupboard, selecting carefully. He fills his glass with water and places it equally carefully beside his placemat. He casts his eye over the hob and looks at his watch.

'Three minutes,' he tells me while he paces up and down.

I want to scream. I want to ram his three minutes down his throat.

He hunches over the table. He sits sideways on his chair and leans over his plate with his weight on his left arm so that his chin is nearly in his food. With the fork in his right hand he shovels it in. He makes dreadful noises when he's eating. Gulping for air, like he's drowning. Stuffing his mouth so full his cheeks bulge. Swallowing with a whimper. I can't look. He's up and helping himself to seconds before I've finished half of mine. I'm relieved when he goes to switch on television.

I'm not interested in his choice of programmes and I can feel myself growing angry again as he flicks through the channels. He sits directly in front of the screen, pointing with the remote. Flick, click. He watches something for two minutes. Points again. Flick, click. Two minutes more. Flick, fucking click.

I go to bed early with my book.

Over the weekend he reminds me what my domestic duties are. He goes through the cupboards and tells me what we're running out of. Says the tomato passata I bought in the discount store doesn't taste as good as the usual brand. He explains the route I should drive to get to the supermarket and goes into detail about traffic lights and speed cameras. Offers to draw me a diagram.

'I don't need a diagram,' John,' I tell him. 'I've been there hundreds of times. Why are you telling me how to get to the supermarket?'

'Because I know a better way,' he says.

He stands behind me as I'm loading the washing machine. I can feel his stare. I turn around.

'What?' I ask him.

'Which programme are you using, Helen? Do you make use of the thirty minute cycle and low temperature?'

I just nod.

'Keep a look out when they're on the line, Helen. The forecast says rain this afternoon.'

I force a smile. 'Yes,' I say. 'I heard it on the radio.'

He hovers over Sunday lunch preparation. Watches me grating rind for lemon meringue. He presses the timer on the oven to see how many minutes the pastry case still needs.

'It has to come out of the oven in eleven minutes, Helen. If it takes a further fifteen for the baking beans to cool down, that means you've got twenty six minutes to make the lemon filling and whip up the egg whites. Then you can remove the beans and fill the pastry case. Are you running late, Helen? Have you made Yorkshire puddings? The batter needs to stand.'

'I know the batter needs to stand, John. It was me who told you the batter needs to stand.'

'I saw green beans in the fridge, Helen. And sweet potatoes. They'll be good with roast lamb. I'd like some Crème Fraîche with my lemon meringue. Did you remember to buy Crème Fraîche, Helen? I didn't see that in the fridge.'

He looks at his watch.

'Twenty five minutes now,' he says.

Shrieking obscenities fill my thoughts. *For fuck's sake, shut the fuck up.*

'John,' I say with another forced smile. 'Would you take these out to the dustbin, please?'

He takes the rubbish and through the kitchen window I watch him walking down the garden path to the compost heap. Sometimes he prances like a pony when he walks. When he's pleased with himself, he lifts up onto his toes and does a funny walk. I can see he's pleased with himself. I know there's going to be a lecture on sorting rubbish into recyclables and compost material when he comes back.

Later, he sits sideways at the table and gulps. He gulps louder over the lemon meringue.

Thursday comes around again and I go to my second meeting. Watery sunlight glistens on wet school walls. In the small classroom the tables have been pushed to one side; chairs arranged in a semicircle. I'm the last one to arrive. The room is warm but I'm shivering. I haven't slept well. John has complained this morning about the smell of my perfume and my nerves are shot.

The women are in their usual places. I recognise a few faces. Besides Joyce, the group leader, I can remember only two names: Pauline and Christina. I smile at them. They are all smiling and waiting for me. I fix my eyes on the clock. Joyce begins.

'Helen, are you ready?'

I was ready last week. It's hard to begin again. I'm not sure how much I'm going to tell them. I'm worried it will come out all wrong, but I might as well get it over with.

I tell them about my weekend: John's pacing about and timing the cooking; the way he eats; the supermarket route diagram he pinned on the kitchen pegboard showing positions of speed bumps, traffic lights and cameras; his hyper- vigilance around the house. Watching me. Checking on me. Reminding me.

One by one, they gasp.

'You've tried talking to your husband about the things that annoy you?' Joyce says.

'So many times. Years' worth. It makes no difference. I'm wasting my breath.'

One of the women speaks up.

'Stay positive, Helen,' she tells me. 'Don't give up.'

Christina shakes her head and contradicts.

'I'd say she's had enough. How is being more assertive going to help?'

Now that I've started, I feel less nervous. Less worried. I take the floor.

'I thought that being more assertive would help me get the message across. I thought perhaps I wasn't saying it properly, that there was a better way, better words.'

More voices join.

'But, he's such a control freak, isn't he? How long has this been going on?' one asks me.

'Six years.'

'Jesus, I'd have killed him by now.'

'Me, too,' another agrees.

I know now that it's all going to come out. I'm surprised to feel reasonably calm. I listen to them debating, arguing about the right way to deal with him. And so I reach the moment when I tell them. They're not going to like what I say next. This is the point where their expressions will change; encouraging smiles will fade. They'll view the whole thing very differently. And they will judge me.

'John isn't my husband,' I say. 'John is my husband's child. He's twelve.'

I watch them. Just as I expected, their faces fall. Mouths gape, wide yet silent. They look at each other and back at me.

'I needed someone to talk to. Someone to tell,' I say.

The silence persists. Joyce steps in.

'Your husband allows John's behaviour to continue?' she asks.

'Neil doesn't see what I see. He denies there's a problem. He doesn't react. Take last Christmas. John couldn't find his favourite old shirt. I told him it wasn't ironed. I said I didn't think he'd need it on Christmas Day.'

'And he said?"

I look at the expectant faces.

'He said, *I know it's Christmas, but you're still supposed to do the ironing.*'

'And your husband heard him say this to you?'

'Yes. John talks to his father in the same way. Sunday morning, Neil was doing breakfast. John stood behind him with his arms folded and said, *when I say I'll have my bacon at eight thirty, I don't mean eight forty five.* Neil apologised; went into his consolation voice. I told John he shouldn't speak to his father like that. They both looked at me as if I were the one in the wrong. Neil won't say anything to John about his behaviour.'

I can hear the classroom clock ticking.

'Why do you think your husband is so reluctant?' Joyce asks.

I'm bursting to say it. Surely, it's the right thing to do. It's my turn to speak now, to say it all. Let it out. I want them to know. There they all sit, eyes wide, and I know what they're thinking. But they can't begin to understand until I explain.

'Neil can't say no to his son. It goes back before I met him.'

I can see them settling in for the story. My head is clear and the words flow.

'John was only three years old when his mother died. When I met Neil two years later, John was a very anxious child. He wanted everything to stay the same. He was afraid of anything new. He constantly checked his father's whereabouts. It's understandable. The worst thing that could happen to a young child had already happened and John tried to control everybody and everything to stay safe. Not being in control was a scary place for him to be.

'Poor little thing,' Pauline says.

'So everybody in his wider family gave in to him. He always got his own way. He used tantrums to get what he wanted. He still does. His father has always let him have what he wants.

I can see they're perplexed. They don't know how to react. Joyce helps me along.

'And he still tries to control everything?'

'Yes. I think he's forgotten the root of his anxieties, but it's like they're programmed into his head. He is so wary of change. He still likes to keep things the same.'

'Can I say something?' somebody asks. 'My neighbour's boy is like that. He goes ballistic if anybody moves his things. He has lots of routines and rituals, too. He's been diagnosed with something.'

I know what she's talking about.

'I've looked into that. Thank you for your suggestion. You might be right. Sometimes I do think John may have some kind of condition. I wouldn't want to put a label on him. It's much more complicated because he was a bereaved child. It's hard to know which behaviour is because he can't help it and which is born out of his fears.'

'Or just a child being arsey,' Christina suggests.

'Poor boy,' Pauline says again.

'That's what I used to think. Poor child. I wanted to help him. And Neil. I thought I could make a difference but they wouldn't let me in. They kept me out. Kept me separate. John and his dad made arrangements together; decided household things together. I couldn't even move the furniture without a scene.'

I can't stop now. It's flooding out.

'I started speaking up. Pointing out inappropriate behaviours. Sometimes it felt like John was the parent and Neil was the child. Neil never backed me. It was always left to me to deal with the tough stuff. Mine was the negative voice in the house, me against them. They marginalised me even more and I knew I had to break the pattern. So I shut up. I let it all happen around me. But I can't stand it any more and I'm not sure what to do next.'

Joyce shifts in her seat.

'But John's just a child, Helen. You're the grown-up.'

I glance around the room. Eyes are not so gentle now; expressions less benign.

'Let me ask you all something,' I say. 'When you thought John was my husband, you sympathised. I saw your faces. You were cringing. When I told you about last weekend, it made you angry. Why is it different now that you know he's only twelve?'

Pauline shakes her head in disbelief.

'Because he *is* only twelve. He's just a boy. It's not his fault.'

'I know it's not his fault,' I say. 'But one day he will be a man. And he's already well on the way to turning into the kind of man none of you could stand. How will he find his place in the world? At work? In relationships? He'll drive people crazy.

Joyce coughs.

'Maybe you can't stop that from happening, Helen.'

'I've got to try. Isn't that what parents are supposed to do?'

'How do you mean?" Pauline asks.

I'm feeling like a case study, but I carry on.

'I've got to break some of his habits. For his sake. Sabotage his routines. Put him out of his comfort zone.'

Pauline's eyebrows hit the ceiling.

'That's monstrous,' she says. 'You're saying you plan to deliberately hurt him. Mothers don't do that to their children.'

Christina supports me.

'Pauline,' she says. 'I think Helen's right. The kid's trapped. He's stuck in old patterns. Somebody's got to help him get out. It's obvious her husband can't do it. What choice has she got?'

An argument ensues about Neil's role. Joyce has to intervene.

'Helen, you said at first you didn't know what to do. It seems, however, that you do indeed have a plan. I think this certainly shows assertiveness. But, I have to say from what you've told us, it isn't going to be easy. Can you tell us more about your plans?'

Except for Christina's encouraging expression, I feel I'm on my own, but I plough on.

'I'm not going to be party to his habits any more. I'm going to challenge them. I'm going to be unpredictable. I plan to let him experience the discomfort of not being in control of me so he can learn how to cope with it.'

'He'll hate it, and he'll hate you,' Pauline says. 'What gives you the right to put him through that pain?'

There's no time to answer her. The bell rings. I have taken up the whole of the session. Schoolchildren push along the corridor and race across the forecourt to the waiting buses. In the classroom we pull back the tables into rows and stack chairs for the evening cleaners. I can sense that most of the women can't wait to talk about me. I know they'll go home and discuss me with their husbands. More than ever, I feel like a wicked stepmother.

Christina waits for me to gather my things.

'Fancy a coffee before you go home?' she says.

I look out the window at the darkening sky. John will start pacing soon. But, I have to make a start somewhere.

'Yes, I do. Thank you for asking,' I say.

In the coffee bar, Christina sees me looking at my watch.

'Forget it,' she tells me. 'You're allowed to do something for yourself, you know.'

It feels strange. It's so long since I did anything *different*.

'Come on,' she says. 'Tell me what you're going to do when you get home.'

I am pathetically grateful for her concern.

'I won't be in the kitchen at inspection time tonight. Dinner is going to be late. Afterwards, *I'll* choose something to watch on television *and* hold onto the remote.'

'Sounds good to me, girl,' she says with a nod. 'Can I ask you something?'

'Go ahead.'

'Didn't you see the problems before you got married? I mean, I would have run a mile, Helen. I've got to be honest with you.'

My insides flip. A prickling sensation rises from somewhere deep down. It runs along my arms and makes my fingers tingle. Heat stabs at my face, my ears, my eyes. My throat tightens.

'We're not married,' I tell her.

'What?'

'We were going to. We were supposed to. It just never happened. Neil wanted to wait until he felt John was ready.'

Christina slumps in her seat.

'Oh, Helen,' she says. 'Six years?'

Her tone of voice is the one you use when a puppy has soiled the floor again. The strength and determination I felt in the classroom is gone and the tingling sensation takes over. I feel foolish. Christina straightens up and stares at me.

'Helen,' she says. 'Why are you putting up with this shit? Get out of it, girl. Go. Get your life back. Leave them to it. I'm so angry for you.'

My walk home takes me past the bus station. With every step my face burns hotter. I don't feel the chill of the evening air; I haven't bothered to fasten my coat. Bus queues of people are happy to be going home. They're laughing. I can't remember the last time I laughed like that. I can't remember the last time I had a good night's sleep. I've forgotten why I thought I could make a difference in John's life.

I turn the corner into our road. I stride up to the house with my coat flapping open. I'm trembling, shaking. I'm getting my words ready for them. My face is cold now; my insides like a stone. My teeth feel wet. It's as if all the tears I never cried have gathered in my mouth as spit to mix with the words I want to spew. I open the back door.

I'm too late. Pieces of pizza are strewn all over the kitchen. Drawers have been pulled out from the units, their contents scattered. Plates lie smashed where they've been thrown. Neil is cowering on the floor in the corner by the radiator. John is beating him over the head with one of the empty drawers.

'I have pizza on Fridays!' he is yelling at his father. Neil's hair is matted with blood. More blood pours from a gash on his temple where John has side-swiped him.

Neil lifts his arms to cover his head from the blows. The drawer comes down and smashes into pieces. John looks around. His face is contorted with rage.

The pizza cutter is on the worktop. I slide it towards John's reach and step back outside into the cool night.

*CO*ARSE *from the Oxford Dictionary*
rude or vulgar (of a person or their speech)

BITTERS AND SOCKERS

August 1982

I liked talking to Janice. She wasn't the same as the other women on the twilight shift.

They clock on just before five and come swooping through the rubber vulcanising shed like a flock of waddling geese, all chatter and noise, high heels and handbags clacking and flapping through the gangways. The men whistle and shout things as the women pass. Some of the girls leer back. They cheer for the best defined, shining bare chest. It's as hot as a sauna in the vulcanising. Our workroom is on through the back of the factory building. It's only just a bit cooler there.

We make slippers at J.B. King. The vulcanisers weld the rubber sole to the uppers. When the racks have cooled, it's one of my jobs to wheel them through for the women in the finishing department. We don't put a J.B. King label on them because most of our product goes to a well-known high street chain. We put *their* labels on the socks. That's what they call the soft inner sole.

I came to earn some money before I go back to sixth form college after the summer break. Uncle Malik helped get me the job. He's night foreman in the vulcanising. They're mostly Asians in there on the night shift. Malik is my father's youngest brother; he isn't thirty yet. He's popular with everybody and I know my father is proud of him. The English women say he's good-looking.

'You'll be fine, Ahmed,' he said to me. He put his hand on my back the way my father does sometimes. 'Take your head out of your books. Learn about the real world. I'll speak to Mrs Charlton about it. I know she's looking for extra hands to help with Christmas orders.'

Mrs Charlton, the HR woman trusts his judgement. So did I. When he told me I'd find the work educational I didn't fully realise what he meant. I assumed he was referring to the whole business model. Learning from shop floor experience. Raw material to finished product. Time and management skills. The women on the twilight shift had other ideas.

Christmas orders have to be delivered by the end of August. That's how it works with the big names on the high street. J.B.King is at full stretch and there are big bonuses to earn. It's piece-work. The more you do, the more bonus you're paid. In our workroom the women aim to finish ten racks of slippers during their four hour shift. There are ten shelves each side of a rack, ten pairs on each shelf. That's four thousand times they bit, or sock and glue. Their hands fly through the actions, fingers stretched like a pianist's. Their bodies rock and sway with the rhythm of the work. It's like a line dance.

Janice used to be a bitter. On my first night's work she was the only one who smiled at me. I asked her to explain what she was doing.

'See this?' she said, showing me the knife in her hand. 'I have to take off the extra bit of seam left over from the vulcanising. Watch.'

She shoved her left hand into a slipper, flicked her right wrist to cut off the protruding piece of rubber at the toe, twisted her arm and nipped off the bit sticking out at the back.

'I can only do it one at a time,' she said, 'but look at the other girls. They can hold up a pair and bit both slippers together.'

'Is that a special knife?' I asked.

She laughed. 'It used to be my favourite peeling knife. I brought it from home. They don't give you a knife. You have to bring your own.'

The woman by her side snapped without looking up.

'Janice, for fuck's sake, will you stop gassing and get on? You're falling behind again.'

'Sorry, Debbie,' my new friend said and rolled her eyes at me.I mumbled an apology and moved away. From behind a stand of racks I watched the two women working together. Janice slid her bitted pairs of slippers along the work table to the woman on her right. Debbie, the socker then passed the inner socks over a latex-filled roller, stuffed them inside the slippers and placed the finished pairs on a circular turntable at the end of the work station. When the turntable was full, Janice had to run around the back of Debbie and load the slippers onto an empty rack ready for bagging and boxing. Every now and then I heard Janice call out numbers.

'Ten more pairs ladies' sixes.'

'Last ten pairs ladies' fives.'

I could see that Janice was struggling to keep up. Her blouse was wet with perspiration and she kept a hanky up her sleeve to wipe away the moisture on her face. She was a plump lady compared with the others. It made her out of breath running back and forth, bending and stretching to fill up the racks. But I preferred her roundness to the thin, loud-mouthed Debbie. Janice was the type of lady you'd like for your mum. She'd make children feel safe and happy.

'Rack of men's coming up. Twenty pairs elevens,' Janice called out and Debbie took down the socks from the pigeon-holes in front of her.

Another of my jobs is to keep the pigeon-holes stocked up with all the different sock sizes for all the gluers. Then I wheel the completed racks into the bagging and boxing department in the next room, ready for shipping.

I was surprised, on that first night, in those noisy, hot rooms with the smell of glue and hot rubber. I didn't know that English people worked in sweat shops, too.

On my second night, there was a different bitter working in Janice's place. I went to ask Debbie.

'Why do you want to know? Fancy giving her one, College Boy? Like little fatties, do ya?' she said.

Both of the women laughed with a horrible grating sound and elbowed one another in the ribs.

'Here, love,' the other one said to me. 'I've never 'ad a bit of black. Come over to the toilets and show me your cock.'

My face burned. They sniggered through their noses. I thought they were disgusting. I found Janice later, on her own in the mending corner.

'I can't keep up with Debbie,' she told me. 'So the supervisor's put me here.'

'By yourself? All night?'

She nodded. 'Well, I suppose it's only fair. If I can't work fast enough, Debbie can't earn her bonus.'

'So what do you have to do here?' I asked.

'Fix up these seconds and make them look better. Smooth out the bubbles in the rubber. They sell them on the markets.'

'What about *your* bonus?'

'There isn't one on this job. It's flat rate.'

I looked at the small space where she'd been put to work. Surrounded by racks of materials and tubs of fluids, she had a little table and a battered chair next to a wall socket where she plugged in her soldering iron.

'They should give you a better light. It's dark in this corner.' I said.

'Yes, but it's cooler back here. And nobody can see me behind all these stock shelves,' she said with a little shrug of her shoulders.

As I passed in and out of the vulcanising, collecting racks, picking up supplies at the the sock bins and on into the boxing, the rows of bitters and sockers worked furiously to the tempo of the music piped through the rooms. From the start of the evening twilight shift, the same music looped through television theme tunes like Hawaii-Five-O or Abba's number ones, the women singing along, hands flying, shoulders and rumps twisting and swaying.

'College Boy!' they called after me. 'Come and give us a kiss.'

Janice sat alone in the mending corner, head bowed over her work, hot iron in her hand. She had a book propped up against a box in front of her. From time to time she looked up to read. I was curious. I made sure all the pigeon-holes were full, racks stacked in correct places and wandered over.

Over her shoulder, I read aloud the title of the book, 'Using Lotus 1,2,3.'

'Ahmed,' she said. 'Don't creep up on me like that. You made me jump.'

'Sorry, Janice. Should you be doing that while you're at work?'

'No. And if they find out, I'll get the sack.'

She must have read my inquisitive face.

'I'm learning how to use spreadsheets,' she said. 'But I don't understand how to link pages.'

It felt good to be able to tell her, 'I can help you with that.'

I went to her house the following Saturday afternoon when her husband was at home.

'Come in, Ahmed,' he greeted me at the door. I felt like an honoured guest. They offered me tea and took me upstairs to their spare bedroom where they kept the computer.

They both learned quickly and offered to pay me. Of course I refused.

'No thank you,' I said. 'I offered to help. I didn't expect payment.'

They told me they were planning to start a baby care business, but I couldn't see any evidence of children in the house. We took our tea into their sitting room. On the sideboard there were framed photographs of two bright-eyed little boys with identical blond haircuts. Janice saw me looking.

'They look just like you,' I said.

'Yes, they did,' her husband replied as Janice moved off to fetch biscuits. His voice wavered. His words came out in short gasps. 'Twins . . . beautiful boys . . We lost them. Spina Bifida. Died on the same day . . . minutes apart . . . just the same way they came into the world.' He shook his head as if he still couldn't believe it.

His shoulders drooped. 'There'll be no more children. No, there's no need to say anything. You didn't know.'

I clamped my mouth closed around my shortbread biscuit and chewed slowly. I thanked them for the refreshments and made my way to the front door. Janice put her hand on my shoulder.

'Don't tell anybody, Ahmed, please. About our business plans. I don't want any of that lot at work to know.'

'Of course not,' I told her.

I walked along the avenue, admiring the smart houses with their carefully kept front gardens. I wanted a place like that, one day. When I got home Uncle Malik was with my father.

'Here he is,' my father said. 'Where have you been?'

I told them.

'It's not a good idea, Ahmed,' my father said.

'Your father is right, my boy. People will talk.'

'Talk about what?' my mother said as she came in with drinks and snacks on a tray. I repeated what I'd just said. She put her hand over her mouth and stood, staring at me.

'What did I do that's so wrong?' I asked them.

They related tales I'd heard before: what it used to be like for them when they were children; what it was like for their parents who were the first generation to move to England. I shook my head.

'It's not the same now,' I argued. ' We can have friends anywhere, Dad. They don't have to be the same as us to be good people. How can you be so old-fashioned?'

They wouldn't settle until I'd promised not to go to Janice's house by myself again.

When the evening shift women came in the next Monday, the trouble began. One passed around a wallet of photographs and the rest gathered to have a look.

'College Boy!' Debbie shouted. 'Come and look at this.'

All the women were sniggering and I didn't want to look but one of them grabbed me and another pushed the picture under my nose.

'This is you, College Boy,' Debbie said. 'Coming out of Janice's house. Look, she's got her hand on your shoulder. Give her a good one, did ya?'

'I helped with her computer. Let go of me.'

'Went upstairs, you did. Tina saw ya.'

'The computer's upstairs,' I said.

I didn't get it. Why were they trying to make something out of my visiting Janice at her home? The one called Tina grabbed the paper wallet and held out a different picture.

'That looks like a satisfied smile to me, College Boy,' she said, stabbing at the photo with her finger. 'I was at my mother's, wasn't I?' she told the women. 'She's just come back from Benidorm. Her house overlooks Janice's. You can see right in. Couldn't believe it when lover boy here turns up. Well, my mother's camera was on the table by the window and there was still some film left. So I grabbed it, didn't I? In he goes, straight upstairs. No messing about. Husband as well. That must have been an interesting threesome.'

I looked at the women's laughing faces. They were ugly. All of them. Their lips pulled back over their teeth in wide, leering grimaces. Big, red clown lips; pale, cruel eyes. Several of them pushed me to the floor. I fell onto my backside.

'You like white skin, College Boy? Let's give him some, girls,' one egged on the others.

They sat on me and pinned me on the floor. It makes me feel foolish to recall how I wasn't able to shift them. There were too many bodies on top of me. I started shouting. Maybe the supervisor would come and stop them.

One of the women pulled off her top. Her bra looked too small for her; her breasts overflowed in front and at the sides. She thrust her hand inside a cup and pulled out the wobbling flesh with its blue veining and enormous brown nipple. I closed my eyes.

'Suck on this, College Boy,' she ordered me. 'I'll show you what a real woman likes.'

I kept my eyes closed and shouted louder. The woman pulled my head towards her and forced her floppy flesh against my face. I didn't like the smell. It was a sour smell, like baby sick.

'Get off him. Now!' a voice screamed behind me. *Janice.*

'What's up, love? Don't want to share?'

'You heard me. Leave him alone.'

'And what do ya think you're gonna do about it?'

I didn't see what happened next, but my head was forced forwards by a weight from above me. The flabby-breasted woman fell back with a shriek. More of them screamed. High-pitched screeching resonated round me. There was blood on my face and I felt sick. I heard feet running; felt the group back away from me. When I opened my eyes, Janice and Uncle Malik were standing over me. Janice had her bitting knife in her hand.

At first, I thought Janice had attacked the woman, but when my head cleared, I saw that Janice's knife was clean; there was no blood on it. The blood was on me. And down the front of the woman. I had bitten her. I had bitten my tongue as well. Lunging for the woman, Janice had over balanced and fallen across the top of my head. Forced into the woman's flesh, my teeth had snapped together and taken a lump out of the disgusting creature. I don't like to think about it now.

Uncle Malik drove me home. Mother wrapped a bag of frozen peas in a tea towel to hold against my sore cheek. We sat with my father in mother's best room.

'I can't go back there,' I lisped with my swollen tongue.

'You must. It's your job. Your responsibility. You did no wrong, Ahmed,' Malik said.

'I can't face them.'

'You lose all face if you don't.'

My father nodded his agreement. Mother sat quietly. Father got up and stood with his back to the fireplace.

'You will go back to work tomorrow,' he said. 'Show them you are strong. You are the victim here, my son. There will be recriminations, but not against you. Their behaviour was intolerable.'

I took a shower before going to my room. I could hear them talking in low voices before Malik returned to his night shift.

When I walked into the workroom on Tuesday night, the women were working in silence. I didn't look at them as I stocked up their sock bins. They thanked me politely. Debbie wasn't in her usual place and I couldn't see Janice anywhere either. I was nervous moving about around the women, but I tried to remember what my family had told me.

'Hold your head up, Ahmed,' they said. 'Go about your business as if nothing has happened. Don't be unfriendly, nor too friendly either. Be efficient. Do your job.'

I repeated those words in my head as I moved from room to room. I saw Malik watching me from the office window in the vulcanising. He smiled and nodded to encourage me. I wanted to ask someone about Janice but I didn't really want to catch the eye of any of the women.

While I was collecting sock supplies from the big containers in the stockroom, the supervisor came to have a word.

'I'm sorry about what happened last night. You can rest assured nothing like that will ever happen again,' she said.

She didn't give me chance to respond. She went straight on.

'Janice Wilson has been dismissed for her attack on a work colleague. I've spoken to your uncle and he confirms that your family doesn't want to put in a formal complaint. I think that's best. Best forgotten.'

She walked away in the direction of the boxing room and I wanted to shout after her.

That's all wrong, I wanted to say. *That's not fair*, I wanted to scream like a child.

My face went hot and I burned inside with anger. I went to the toilet to splash water on my face. Cooler and composed, I went to confront my uncle.

'Be still,' he told me. 'There is nothing to be gained by making a fuss.'

'But, it's not fair,' I argued. 'I was the one who was attacked. They forced me . . .'

'Ahmed, come into my office.' I followed him and he asked me to close the door behind me. 'Those women are foolish jokers. They tease the new boys. You're not the first.'

I stared hard at him.

'You mean, you knew something like this would happen?'

He looked down at his hands.

'Not quite like this. They went too far this time.'

I slammed the door behind me as I left the office. The glass panes rattled. I worked in a rage through the rest of the evening. I saw the women collecting their things towards the end of their shift and was surprised to see Debbie coming out of the mending corner. It had been empty when I'd gone there looking for Janice earlier. I ducked back behind some racks to listen.

'Fuckin' stupid,' I heard her say. 'Anyway, they won't keep me there for long, Carol. They know I'm the fastest and the best. Next time there's a rush on. You'll see.'

They linked arms like lovers and sauntered through the vulcanising. laughing and joking, dipping into their handbags for cigarettes they'd light up as soon as they got outside.

The woman I'd bitten didn't come back for a week and when she did, the supervisor teamed her with Debbie who came out of the mending corner with a real swagger.

'What did I tell ya, girls? I knew it wouldn't last long.'

My insides boiled. I hated her.

We had a new design to work with. Extra frilly high-heeled mules, trimmed in satin with bows, fluffy feathers and other fancy stuff. Santa specials. *Boudoir Beauties*, they were called. Debbie was furious. She wasn't selected to work with the team on the hot glue guns.

'You're needed here,' the supervisor told her. 'Nobody socks as fast as you.'

High-heeled mules don't have the same kind of inner as regular flat soled slippers. The shape of the whole thing comes ready moulded in a hard kind of plastic. There's no vulcanising to do because there's no rubber content. You don't need bitters either. A different team of women stick down the outer textile to the framework. They work foot pedals while hot glue squirts from guns clamped to their work tables. They do their own racking and unracking and they don't have time to talk and tease people. They can't take their eyes off the boiling hot glue so close to their hands. Not for a second.

I saw Debbie staring at finished racks of fancy slippers as I wheeled them through for boxing. She looked jealous. I turned my head away and smiled.

On Friday night she came into work all dressed up. So did the flabby woman. I heard them saying they were going out on the town after work. They took their overalls out of their bags and slid the handbags under the work station. They called me over.

'Everything all right now, love?' Debbie said to me. 'All forgotten, eh?'

I nodded and moved away. I'd *never* forget what they'd done to me. I wished I could stick their heads under the glue guns. I wished I could staple the lips of their dirty mouths together. I shrugged off those bad thoughts and concentrated on my work, knowing September and college wasn't so far away.

Later they called me again. I was on my way to the boxing with a rack full of Boudoir Beauties.

'Ahmed, here love. Can you sort out these sock sizes for me? I think some of them are in the wrong places.'

I'm always careful when I'm restocking the pigeon-holes. I know I don't make that kind of mistake, but I went to check anyway. Debbie stayed right up close beside me and I knew she was pretending to bc nice.

'Must be my eyesight, love,' she said when I showed her everything was as it should be. 'But, thank you anyway. Weekend at last, eh? Going anywhere good?'

I found my voice and some courage.

'I wouldn't tell you if I was. Don't pretend to be my friend. It's never going to happen.'

I turned to move off and out of the corner of my eye I saw the other one straightening up from bending under the table. She tried to hide what she was doing but I guessed what was happening. I pretended I'd seen nothing and went on my way. Two pairs were missing from the rack and under their work station their bags bulged.

I went straight to see my uncle. Someone from the canteen was in the office with him. She stepped away from his side as I came in. There was lipstick on his face.

'Is Mrs Charlton still here?' I said.

'I doubt it. Why?'

'What's the penalty for stealing slippers?'

'Instant dismissal. Why?'

I was too breathless to answer him properly. My head and heart were pounding with the rush of realising I had found a way to pay Debbie back. It might not be as satisfying as hot glue and staples, but I couldn't let this chance slip by.

'Do you have authority to call a bag search, Uncle?'

He looked puzzled but he nodded.

'You must search bags tonight as the women leave,' I said.

The canteen woman sucked in a breath and made a whistling noise. Malik took her to the office door.

'Kathleen,' he said to her. 'You know you must say nothing.'

She put her finger to her lips, picked up an empty tray and went out. Malik looked troubled.

'Debbie?' he said.

‘Yes. And the other one.’

‘Leave it with me.’

Just before the women were due to finish, I made an excuse to go outside. I went to the supervisor and told her I was feeling very hot and needed some air. I leaned against the factory wall, watching the main entrance, waiting to see what happened. Uncle Malik arrived with the supervisor and another woman. I planned to step forward and let Debbie see me as she was caught. I wanted to smile into her lying, cheating face. I looked forward to tasting her downfall.

She appeared in the doorway with the other one. They opened their bags for inspection, got out their cigarettes and lit up. They walked out into the yard, arms linked. As they reached the gate, Debbie turned back to wave.

‘See ya later, Malik,’ she called. ‘Maybe I’ll have something hot waiting for ya.’

The two women laughed with that same coarse throatiness I had come to detest. Malik didn’t want to speak to me. He waved me away but I followed him to his office.

‘You warned them,’ I accused him. He didn’t look at me. I thrust my face right into his. “How could you?’

‘Don’t raise your voice to me, Ahmed. I am your family. Show some respect.’

I couldn’t believe what he had allowed. My senses were on fire. I didn’t know you could feel so many emotions at the same time. I raged at the injustice of his actions. His betrayal sickened me. He’d denied my own suffering for his own selfish reasons. I could hardly bear to look at him. I stood over him as he sat at his desk and I watched his face as he fought to keep the upper hand.

‘Go away, little boy. I have work to do.’

I would not let him dismiss me that way. I tried to sound like my father as I gathered myself.

‘You owed it to me, Uncle. You owed it to Mrs Charlton. Most of all, you owed it to Janice.’

His head tilted to the side and he looked at me as if I had no sense at all.

'Janice isn't my girlfriend,' he said.

My stomach knotted. A bitter taste rose in my mouth and I wanted to hit him. I stood my ground and waited until he was forced to look at me again. I kept my voice calm and soft.

'Thank you for teaching me about the real world,' I said.

In his eyes, I saw a little flicker of fear. I took away with me some satisfaction that he didn't know what I planned to do next.

UNREHE*ARSED from Collins Dictionary*
not having been practised in advance

THE END OF THE WORLD PARTY

There were thirteen of us including Henry. Henry said it was appropriate. Like a *Last Supper* before the Mayan calendar ran us all out of time, out of the galaxy, the universe, whatever. His house is in Bugarach, the Languedoc village in the news for its upside down mountain and mysterious prophecies.

'It'll be different, Paul,' he told me, his sing-song Welsh accent more pronounced than ever. 'Oh, yes. I can guarantee it'll be different.'

I could hear excitement in his voice. If the prophecies proved correct, Bugarach would be one of only two safe places in the world after midnight on the twenty first of December. I thought it was bunkum. I could see no connection between the ancient Mayan civilisation and its calendar and a village in southern France. The rock formations of the mountain were interesting but not unique. The whole region was dotted with volcanoes long extinct. Cathar strongholds occupied the heights, villages perched high on cliffs above the hinterland, safe from the prying eyes of religious persecution. On the coast there was black volcanic sand on some beaches. There may have been upside down mountains in other places, too. But, Bugarach had made the most of its oddities and lovers of mysteries, like Henry, revelled in making these tenuous connections with all things other-worldly.

'Who was that on the phone?' My sister, Julia was standing behind me.

'Henry,' I said with a smile, imagining Henry's large, round face full of the joy of his favourite subject.

‘Oh, *him*. What did he want?’

‘We’re invited to a party in Bugarach on the twenty first.’

She sniffed and said,

‘You’ve told him no thank you, of course.’

She was wearing her headmistress face, the one with chin raised, lips pressed tight together. My stomach cramped at the tone of her voice.

‘Actually, Julia, I’ve told him we’ll be there.’

‘Oh, Paul. The place will be full of crackpots.’

She frowned.

‘I know. Sounds like fun.’

‘And I suppose John and *Carol* will be going?’

‘Yes. I don’t know what’s happened between you two. You used to be good friends.’

‘You know very well what I mean.’

‘You’re wrong about her.’

She humphed and took herself off into the kitchen.

John and his wife Carol were the ones who’d introduced Julia and me to the choir where we all sang. We’d grown close through rehearsals and concerts, socials, sharing nights out and so on. Julia seemed to think Carol wanted to get too close. She said Carol hung on my every word.

‘Haven’t you noticed?’ Julia once asked me. ‘She’s flirting with you. Be careful.’

Julia was quiet at dinner that night. Whenever I tried to instigate a conversation with her she cut me short. After coffee she told me she wanted to read and left me to clear while she went to bed early.

The headmistress face appeared again in the morning, but I ignored it. Henry’s *end of the world* party was something to look forward to. I thought it would do Julia good to get out of the house, be among lively people. It would be good for me, too.

I was *baby brother*, the late surprise addition to the family when mother was in her forties and Julia was fourteen. It turned out I was fussy about food. Julia was the only one who could get me to eat, so the story went, doing the aeroplane spoon thing or pretending to feed wild animals at the zoo while I made the appropriate beastly noises.

She still had an old shoebox full of photographs of the two of us: Julia taking me out in my pushchair; Julia and me sitting on a wall by the sea; Julia and me eating ice creams and pictures of her holding tightly to my plump, little body on fairground rides. She used to say how much she enjoyed having a little brother. It gave her the chance to forget about things like teenage *angst*. She loved having the opportunity to repeat her own favourite childhood things.

Our parents never featured in those old photos. Mother would be behind the camera; Dad would be in the background somewhere, looking on, the pair of them like spectators in the Paul and Julia show. I don't remember either of our parents ever eating ice creams with us on a wall by the sea or going on roller coaster rides and dodgem cars.

After mother died when I was seven, Julia became *sister-mum*. That's what I actually called her when I was little. Later, after we'd lost dad, too, big sister looked after everything. Without Julia, I don't know what would have happened to me.

But, at forty-eight, divorced, and sharing a home with big sister Julia, it wasn't so easy playing baby brother. There were times I wanted to break free and then I'd feel guilty about it. An end of the world party in the French village at the centre of international media interest was a welcome distraction.

Bugarach has an attractive location, off the beaten track, surrounded by virgin country and ancient forests with Pic de Bugarach, the upside down mountain, the highest peak in the Corbières as backdrop. For years the village was associated with alternative thinking, alternative therapies and the like, but the coming apocalypse had seen a huge influx of visitors. I'd heard about some of the problems on the radio, but wasn't expecting the noisy circus we found when we arrived.

We had trouble getting through cordons of police blocking the route. The road was a sea of French blue uniforms and metal barricades.

'But, we're invited to a party here tonight officer,' Julia said in her impeccable French, followed by a sigh.

'I am sorry, Madame,' the gendarme said, 'but as you can see, the village is overcrowded. There are complaints.'

We tended to rely on Julia's superior language skills when we went out as a group. Sometimes, there were more of us: expats, living the dream in a house in the sun, but several had gone to England for Christmas. John and Carol had met us en route and followed in their car. The others were in convoy behind.

'We're not here to make noise or nuisance,' Julia said, but the gendarme shrugged and apologised again.

Behind him, two men climbed out from a tent pitched in a clearing beyond the barrier across the road. One was dressed in a silver outfit and wore a face mask like a Roswell alien. The other one looked like he'd come straight from Chalmun's Cantina in *Star Wars*. His face was painted green and he wore a headdress with rubbery tentacles dangling from it. A woman with a microphone accompanied by a man with an outside broadcast camera rushed up and started asking questions.

'Oh, for goodness' sake,' Julia said as the costumed characters began pulling silly faces for the media and doing funny walks. 'I hope Henry hasn't invited any of *these* people.'

I admired Henry. Nutty as a fruitcake, but great fun to be with. He'd stopped trying to convince me the world was already populated with aliens. He turned up to choir practice and the occasional Bridge afternoon and took his turn at hosting social events. In his fifties, he lived alone. I couldn't imagine anybody putting up with his odd ways and practical jokes on a permanent basis, not to mention sharing a house full of crystal skulls and other so-called evidence that we've been visited before by creatures from outer space.

Julia was still trying to make headway with the boys in French blue. The aliens had been joined by other New Age campers: women with zills on their fingers wearing robes like Druids; a man of indeterminate age with a long, grey beard and another personage of questionable sex, wearing a cycling cape over leather trousers decorated with sleigh bells that jingled in competition with the women's finger cymbals.

'Our friend is waiting for us,' Julia was telling the police, her voice raised against the annoying pinging noises. 'Our friend, Henry Williams.'

' 'Enri? You mean 'Enri Gallois?' the gendarme said.

The finger cymbals pinged faster and one of the women chanted,

' 'Enri Gallois. 'Enri Gallois. Le Gallois. Le Gallois.'

'No, no,' John said. 'That can't be our Henry. Our Henry doesn't smoke. Only a cigar on special occasions. You'd never see him with any of those French fags.'

'*Gallois*,'Julia shouted at him. John's face was a blank. 'Oh, come on, John. Not *Gauloise*. Gallois isn't about cigarettes. It's French for Welsh.'

I cringed. Julia had on *that* voice again. Imperious. I had a lifetime of reasons to be grateful to her, but since her husband died she'd been impossible, trying to control everybody, it seemed to me, as if she could ward off further disasters in her life by keeping a tight rein on everything else.

Living together had worked well for us, in the beginning. My ex had remarried; our son had taken a job abroad; Julia was on her own again. I took up Julia's offer to say with her in France. She was my sister-mum and I loved her, but that condescending way she spoke to people was becoming an issue. She could have made a joke about John's mistake, but instead she'd slipped into bossy mode. I saw Carol's face redden.

Just as we recognised a softening in the gendarme's attitude, Henry showed up. He came hurrying up to the barricades, his hair damp and sticking to his forehead. There was something different about him. He looked fresh and more alive, somehow, *boyish* even. He elbowed his way through the bells and finger cymbals.

'Sorry, everybody,' he said. 'Just got out of the shower. I meant to be here waiting for you. I thought you'd have trouble.'

He had a few words with the gendarme. He sorted it quickly with nods and shrugs, a bit of arm waving and a joke about end of the world weirdos. We had to leave our cars in the heath and Henry led us, like a crocodile of schoolchildren along the road toward the village. Some of the bells and zills fell in behind. We snaked our way, pinging and ringing, upwards through narrow streets.

'Can't you take my arm?' Julia said to me. 'The soles of my shoes are slippery on these stones.'

'Why did you wear them? You knew where we were coming.'

She tutted and said,

'I didn't know we'd be expected to hike for miles. Perhaps we should have all brought backpacks.'

There were reporters and police everywhere. Villagers huddled in groups on their doorsteps to watch our musical procession. Henry called out greetings to them as we passed.

' 'Enry,' one old boy shouted above the clamour. 'What's the rush? Slow down, my friend. It's not the end of the world.' Laughter.

'You never know,' Henry shouted back.

'See you tomorrow.'

'Maybe.'

Julia said, 'Oh, for goodness' sake.'

We dashed on. More people in costume had set up in the street outside the restaurant. There were stalls selling jewellery made of different coloured crystals; sets of hand-carved runes and Tarot cards; astrological charts and something called kinetic colour imaging to read the colour of your aura. Another group camped outside the bar, further along the stretch of the D14, now completely free from traffic but filled with carnival colour and the noise of bells and drumming.

A middle aged woman in a feathery hat was giving what sounded like a lecture, but her words were unintelligible, like an elvish incantation from *Lord of the Rings*.

'Must be affecting passing trade,' John said as we hurried by.

'Nah. Not likely,' Henry said. 'They're making a fortune.'

We passed through Bugarach, beyond the last of the buildings and into open country. Lac de la Vène came into view, Henry's farmhouse right beside the still water, its face turned toward the village below and at its rear, the rocky mass of the peak.

'Hope you remembered to bring torches,' Henry said. 'You'll need them on your way back. There's no lighting up here.'

We skirted the small lake, its water silent and silver in the twilight, pale as death. In contrast, the lights from Henry's undraped windows were golden and welcoming.

'Come in. Come in,' Henry said and we queued up the steps out front and through his open door. 'Here, let me take your coats.'

Tempting smells wafted through the house. Henry always got that right: food. I could smell chicken and pork sausage and knew there'd be an enormous pot of cassoulet bubbling on the hob, rich and juicy, thickened with beans and chick peas.

The coat rack in the hall was already almost full of shower-proofs and fleeces. I found a space for Julia's jacket and quickly hooked my own over a newel post at the bottom of the stairs. My mouth was watering. After the climb to Henry's house, I had an appetite for a large plate of Henry's stew.

The dining room was at the back of the house. We followed Henry through. A wall of glass doors gave a stunning view across heath land to far forests beyond the lake. The rocky peak of Bugarach stood over it all like a sentinel, impervious, majestic. It was hard to take your eyes from it.

Henry opened the Blanquette, champagne in all but name and we stood around in small groups with our glasses of bubbly, catching up with choir news and glancing outside as light faded further and the mountain loomed purple and mysterious in the shadows.

'So why is it upside down?' Carol said. 'It doesn't look upside down to me.'

'Rock formation,' Henry explained as he filled her glass. 'You'd expect the oldest rock to be at the bottom, but it's at the top, as if the whole thing got flipped over.'

'Oh,' she said. 'Have you ever been up to the top?'

'Years ago. You can't go up there now.'

'Why not?'

'Nobody knows the answer to that, Carol. But there's been a military presence in the village for three years now. They'll tell you they're on manoeuvres up there, but nothing more. Ask too many questions and you get short shrift.'

I scanned the rocks for signs of movement, but the mountain gave no clues.

'Well, that's probably all it is then,' Julia said. 'Military manoeuvres. They have to keep them secret, don't they? Why pretend it's anything more than that?'

She still sounded like the schoolteacher she used to be, commandeering the class away from the dangers of getting sidetracked, forcing *her* will on everybody else.

'They won't tell you what the noises are either,' Henry said.

Carol said, 'What noises?'

'Strange noises in the middle of the night. A kind of humming.'

'Humming noises? In the middle of the night?'

John laughed.

'They've got a male voice choir up there, Carol,' he said. 'They'll be rehearsing, getting ready to entertain the aliens when they land.'

'Oh, shut up, John. Can't you take anything seriously?'

He laughed all the more.

'Carol,' he said. 'Didn't you see the airheads down in the village? Didn't you hear the woman in the queer hat talking gibberish?'

‘That would have been Sylvie,’ Henry said. ‘She speaks a language unknown as yet on Earth.’

‘There you are then,’ John went on. ‘What did I tell you? Idiots, the lot of ‘em.’

There was one glass left empty on the table. I did a quick count. Somebody was missing.

‘Henry, I thought you said we’d be thirteen tonight?’ I said.

‘We are. Hang on a minute.’

He went to the kitchen. A woman came back with him. She wore a long flowered skirt and had her hair piled on top of her head, tied up in a twisted scarf. Some strands had come loose and hung in dark corkscrews to her shoulders. Her eyes were even darker than her hair and her skin still carried a late summer tan. She looked a good ten years younger than Henry.

‘I’d like to introduce Madeleine,’ Henry said. ‘Madeleine is eating with us tonight.’

‘Madeleine is *cooking* tonight,’ she said. The look between them surprised me. That one glance gave away so much. It was immediately obvious to me that Henry and Madeleine were an item. They were grinning like teenagers, their eyes locked in a gaze of private intimacy. I wondered when that had started and why Henry hadn’t mentioned her before.

I glanced at Carol. She lowered her eyes and fiddled with her necklace.

‘You all sing with the international choir,’ Madeleine said. ‘I’m very pleased to meet you. I came to your last concert. I particularly enjoyed the Lawrensen. He would have been pleased with your performance.’

‘You know Morgan Lawrensen?’ I said.

‘Yes. I lived in Los Angeles for a time.’

‘What’s he like?’

‘He’s lovely. Very affable.’

‘I thought he’d retreated to some remote island.’

‘Well, he hasn’t cut himself off from the world, if that’s what you mean. Some of us need peace and quiet when we’re working, don’t we?’

I wanted to find out more about this Madeleine: how and where she’d met our Henry; what she thought about his extra-terrestrial inclinations; what it was *she* did that required peace and quiet. She said she needed to check on something in the kitchen and excused herself. Henry said he was going to the fridge for more chilled wine. Julia took my arm. Her grip was almost fierce.

‘Well,’ she said. ‘What do you think about that?’

‘What?’

‘Don’t pretend you don’t know what I’m talking about.’ She gripped me harder. Carol turned away. ‘The mysterious Madeleine. Where’s Henry been hiding her?’

‘I expect we’ll find out later.’

After a refill of Blanquette, Henry seated us, Carol next to me, Julia and John facing us across the table. Then he helped Madeleine bring in the food. I raised a toast to our hosts, to Bugarach and to the end of the world due at midnight. We ate oysters baked in their shells with a crumbly, garlic flavoured topping. When the fizzy wine was gone, Henry poured white, crisp and dry. Conversations grew more animated as our glasses emptied, refilled, emptied again. We talked of the programme our choirmaster had set for the coming season, who was familiar with the music, who wasn’t.

‘Assuming we’re all still here to sing it,’ I said. ‘You know, after midnight and you-know-what.’

‘Quite right,’ Henry said. ‘Nobody knows what’s happening tomorrow.’

I noticed his face was glowing, his eyes bright and twinkling whenever he glance Madeleine’s way. He looked extremely well and as if he’d shed years since the last time I’d seen him. *The power of love*, I thought. I’d seen that look before, although I hadn’t worn it myself for some years.

Julia leaned toward where Madeleine was sitting at the near end of the table.

'This is delicious, Madeleine,' she said. 'So, tell us. How did you meet Henry?'

The room went quiet. We'd all heard Julia's question. Madeleine laughed: a musical tinkle that showed perfect, white teeth and made her eyes sparkle. Henry was sitting at the other end of the table. She flashed him a smile.

'We've know one another forever. Haven't we Henry?'

They stared, one at the other, across the length of the room as if they were the only two people present. Her words hung in the air. We waited. Julia looked non-plussed. Madeleine didn't offer any more information and Henry merely smiled back. When I glanced around, the others seemed perplexed too. They put down their heads and carried on eating.

'Forever,' Henry repeated. He gave a sigh. I looked from him to Madeleine and back again.

Something was going on. Surely, the others had noticed. Henry was planning something. That was a mischievous twinkle in his eye. Maybe one of his practical jokes was on the cards for later and Madeleine was in on it. Whatever it was, and whether or not it had anything to do with the imminent end of the world, I was certain that Madeleine and Henry had a secret.

✦✦✦

I suppose you could say we were an unusual gathering of people at the Languedoc international choir. Living in different villages scattered around the hills of the Hérault and Aude regions of southern France, we met once a week for rehearsals. We held them in public rooms at the market town standing roughly at the centre of our various home locations.

We came from a variety of backgrounds. There were lawyers, architects, schoolteachers, a retired haulage contractor, property developers, oilfield personnel, a hairdresser, ex-police officers, several artists and three writers including me. After rehearsals, we went to one of the bars in the town square. There was little opportunity to get to know others during rehearsal time. For an hour or so afterwards, in the bar, we mingled with members from other sections of the choir so that, gradually, friendship groups formed. The bar proprietor set aside a room for us through winter months. In summer, we'd sit outside in the shade of enormous plane trees, enjoying aperitifs before it was time to go home for supper.

We shared the names of favourite restaurants, the quickest routes to get to wherever, that sort of thing. We didn't often talk about how we financed our lifestyles, living in the French sunshine, but when the subject did come up, I'd know what to expect.

People were always surprised when I told them my author name.

'You're who?' they'd say.

'Camilla Rose.'

'But she's a woman.'

'Actually, no. Here I am.'

'But, Camilla Rose writes for women. She writes *romances*.'

'Almost correct.'

Male friends all reacted in a similar way when I explained there was a bit more to it than a straightforward *boy meets girl* scenario. It made them uncomfortable. I could tell by the sudden slackening of the jaw and look of surprise in their eyes. They'd shift around a bit and not know where to look. Then they'd try to cover up their discomfort by saying something banal, or by changing the subject completely. Men simply didn't know what was an appropriate reaction.

If I'd written action-packed thrillers or murder mysteries, there'd have been a slap on the back and hearty congratulations. Maybe even a discussion of the plot line and a summary of their favourite scenes. But a man who writes romances? What could they talk about with a man who writes women's stories? A man who, unlike most of them, must know women's minds so well?

I was an enigma. I was someone to be wary of. To some, I was an impossibility.

'It's true we're in a minority,' I'd tell them, 'but there are more men writing for women than you might imagine.'

I'd tell them about the conventions I attended, other writers I'd met over the years. How numbers of men writing in the genre continued to grow. They'd look at me in disbelief. And I knew what some of them were thinking and saying behind my back.

A guy who writes women's fiction and lives with his sister? He must be batting for the other side.

Either that, or I must be some predatory type, stalking their women and taking notes. They'd throw a protective arm around their wives and girlfriends as if I were some immediate threat.

On the other hand, female friends were always the most intrigued that Camilla Rose turned out to be Paul Davison with the deep, bass voice in the back row of the choir. It fascinated them.

'How can a man write like that?' they'd want to know.

'I'm a good listener,' I'd tell them. I never let on that maybe if I'd listened to my wife more, paid more attention to her and a bit less to my own ambitions, I might not be single and living with my sister.

My kind of writing made me an outsider, an oddity. Perhaps that was why extra-terrestrially obsessed Henry and I got on so well.

Most choir members were English and the others French, Dutch, German, Canadian, American: forty acquaintances altogether with a common love for music enjoying the challenge of learning something new. On December twenty first, the eve of the end of the world, eleven of us had come to Henry's party out of regard for him, an excellent Welsh tenor, and because some of us felt he might need somebody with him when the witching hour passed and no aliens had come to rescue him from impending doom. Apparently though, I needn't have worried. He had Madeleine.

I don't take notes on the women I meet. There's no need. I have a good memory. Certain feminine traits are burned into it. I watched Madeleine as she entertained her and Henry's guests, saw how she pulled at the loose strand of her hair every now and then and tucked it behind her ear. Her hands were small with long, slim fingers and she kept her nails short and unpolished. I knew from the first moment I saw her come through from Henry's kitchen into the dining room, one day soon I would base a character on a woman who wore the same kind of clothes, a woman who had a way, like Madeleine, of listening to people with her whole face. It showed in her eyes, her mouth and the tilt of her head. She had a way of making the speaker feel special and important. I could sense that as I watched the faces of her dinner guests.

These were some of the things I noticed about women that set me apart from men I knew. I was able to detect sarcasm in a woman's tone. I was aware when she felt ill at ease. I knew how to read between the lines of what women said. I noticed things like their most becoming colours and the best hairstyles for the shape of their faces. To write about these things convincingly, you have to study your subject.

Madeleine had the confidence to wear the things she liked. Her long, flowered skirt wasn't fashionable, but it fit close to her hips and dropped in a slim tube shape to the tips of her shoes. She knew what suited her. Confidence. I admire that in a woman.

Carol was sitting next to me. She helped stack our used starter plates as people passed them down the table. She leaned in close to me and whispered.

'She's lovely, isn't she? I've seen you watching her.'

'Ah, Carol,' I said. 'You know me. I'm always watching.'

'I think she's already spoken for.'

'Yes. I noticed that, too.'

Madeleine cleared the dishes and disappeared into the kitchen again. Henry followed her. Across the table, Julia was in conversation with Carol's husband, John, discussing the merits of one of our regular concert venues. I added my opinion , but Carol had nothing to say. Her eyes were downcast, focused on her wedding ring. She was nervously twisting it around her finger, backwards and forwards, unaware I could see what she was doing.

Henry and Madeleine came back with the main course, the cassoulet I'd smelled earlier. The room filled with its mouth-watering aroma. They placed two large serving bowls of it in the centre of the table and Henry served us. I could hardly wait to taste it.

'This is fantastic, Madeleine,' I said.

Julia approved and said Madeleine must give her the recipe. One by one, the others agreed, but Carol said nothing. Henry opened bottles of *Faugères,* blood red like garnets, a big wine, a symphony in a glass with harmonies you didn't expect. It made your tongue sing and warmed the back of the throat.

One of the other guests, Martin from the baritone section of the choir raised another toast to our hosts. Our glasses emptied and were filled again. Conversations lulled as we ate and drank, then picked up again as people mellowed further.

'Are you going to give us a song tonight, Henry?' Carol asked, the effects of several glasses of wine shining in her eyes, ringing in her voice.

'Have you got an *end of the world* song?' John added. His lip had a sarcastic curl. His eyes were narrowed. He helped himself to more wine. Carol glared at him. Henry ignored John's little dig and said,

'Skeeter Davis 1963, if I remember correctly. Recorded later by the Carpenters among others. Not something I'd like to sing myself. More of a girl's song.'

Madeleine began singing. John's lip uncurled. His eyes widened. He put his elbow on the table and rested his chin on his hands to listen. Everyone listened. She had superb tone, a trained voice if ever I heard one. There was rapturous applause at the end. We were like uninhibited children, fists banging on the table, feet stamping the floor.

John said, 'We could do with a voice like that in the choir. Brava!'

‘Absolutely,’ Baritone Martin added. ‘Henry, can’t you persuade her?’

‘Madeleine knows her own mind,’ Henry said.

Madeleine thanked us and filled her water glass.

‘You’ve sung before,’ I said.

Her smile was a quiet one, the nod of her head barely perceptible.

The lights flickered. They went off, briefly came on again and then stayed off. The thick blackness in the room was as sudden as the abrupt halt in our conversations. You couldn’t see your hand in front of your face. Henry was the first to speak.

‘Bugger. Sit tight, everybody. Leave this to me.’

Henry’s faceless, bodiless voice came from near the far end of the room. He sounded unperturbed, as if power outage was something that happened regularly. I could hear him scrape back his chair and was aware of movement from his end of the table, but my senses were confused in the thick blanket of darkness. I could feel the shift of air as somebody moved past me, but after only a few seconds of complete darkness, I became disoriented and couldn’t be sure where sounds came from. I wondered if this sudden blackout was the explanation for Henry’s mischievous expression I’d noticed earlier. Was this the beginning of Henry’s secret plan?

‘Is this an end of the world party trick?’ I asked into the black hole of Henry’s dining room.

‘No. It’s the bloody box has tripped. We’re on only nine kilowatt supply up here. We must have overloaded the system. Won’t be a minute.’

I heard him leave the room. I could hear footsteps behind me, retreating along the hall and then the opening of the door.

In the dark, we sat still, waiting. There was muttering from the far end of the table. Someone coughed. I couldn’t see a thing. My eyes were open, looking into a great, black nothingness. I strained in attempt to focus on something. It was impossible. I wondered if this was how it felt floating in outer space.

There was a shuffling noise and then the sound of a wine glass falling over.

'I hope that was empty,' I joked. 'I think it's best we don't move a muscle till Henry's fixed the lights.'

For a moment there was complete silence. The room was solid black and felt empty, twelve invisible people sitting around Henry's table as helpless as babies.

'I heard this sort of thing happens a lot in Bugarach,' someone said. 'Magnetic forces or something.'

Another cough. More shuffling sounds. The blackness felt solid as a wall.

'Oh, my God,' a female voice said. 'Look at the mountain!'

Those of us facing the window saw immediately. There were lights outside, flickering through the heath, moving slowly in a line up the mountainside. I heard Carol gasp and felt her reach for my hand. I took it and covered it with my other hand in a gesture of comfort. I hoped she didn't misconstrue my intentions.

'It's nothing,' I said. 'It's people with torches. That's all it is.'

Carol said, 'Why are they going up there in the dark? It's dangerous. You could trip and fall over anything. You could break your leg. Your neck. What on earth do they think they're doing?'

'Listen everybody,' I said, appealing for calm. 'It's just a bunch of loonies hoping to see what happens. They're going up as far as they can because they think the rocks are going to open up.'

'What do you mean?' Carol said, gripping tight hold of my hand.

'It's the local legend. This is what the end of the world thing is all about. People believe there's some kind of hidden cave up there. When the rocks open up, a spaceship is going to come out and rescue believers.'

John laughed.

Julia said, 'Ridiculous.'

Carol was still gripping tightly onto me.

'What if the rocks really do open? Like an earthquake or something. Why would anybody want to be right in the way of it?' she said.

I said, 'Because they believe whatever is hidden in the mountain will take them away to safety as the world ends.'

'Ridiculous,' Julia said again.

We saw the lights growing more distant as we sat, motionless, watching in silence, still in the pitch dark. Glimmering, guttering, the procession of lights climbed on, further, higher. Then, slowly the lights moved toward each other and came together in a group. The glow lit up a small patch of mountainside, shimmering through the scrub. I felt a shiver run up the back of my neck. There was a distant humming noise. I felt Carol stiffen.

'Isn't that the noise Henry told us about?' she said. 'Humming noises? In the middle of the night?'

'I don't like this,' Julia's voice from across the table, high-pitched and unsure, not sounding so pompous now. 'I wish I'd never come. I knew something like this would happen. Where the hell is Henry?'

The humming sounds grew louder and changed pitch. Two notes repeated. High and lower, high and lower. Over and over. The crescendo swelled, louder and faster and then abruptly stopped. We waited in silence. I could hear someone's shallow breathing.

The house lights flickered back on. People sighed their relief. Carol pulled her hand away from mine.

'Henry,' I said, twisting around to face the door. 'You're back.'

But he wasn't. Madeleine wasn't in her seat either.

Julia said, 'Oh, for goodness' sake.'

I got up and hurried to the kitchen. It was empty. I ran through the other rooms. Martin joined me. The utility room off the kitchen was empty as was the living room.

'Should I look upstairs?' Martin said.

I nodded.

'I'll check outside,' I said.

I grabbed my mobile phone from my coat in the hall and switched on the torch beam. I rushed outside, ran down the steps and into the basement where I assumed the power supply came in.

Henry's basement was full of piles of storage boxes, old bicycles and gardening tools, grey and ghostly in the beam from my torch. There was a phantom workbench in the gloom and a set of skeletal metal shelves. I found the electricity control box on the wall near the door, intact, and as far as I could tell, in perfect working order. I ran my hand over all the switches to check their positions. Everything seemed as it should. I flashed my torch across the floor and walls. I didn't know exactly what I was looking for in the shadows, but there was nothing that stood out as being unusual or out of place.

I found a switch for the basement strip light and flicked it on. The fluorescent tube light pinged, spluttered and settled. Shadows disappeared. The basement and its contents looked normal in the cold glow of the strip light. I switched off my torch and looked around. The workbench was tidy; Henry's power tools were neatly stacked on a rack; gardening equipment leaned against the far wall. The floor was recently swept: there were no dusty footprints. I switched off the light, closed the door and went back inside to the others.

'Where is he?' Julia said as I came into the hall.

'I don't know.'

We gathered in Henry's dining room. Henry's table was strewn with plates of our unfinished meal. Baritone Martin was helping his wife mop up wine spilt during the blackout. John was helping himself to more from the bottle. Carol was scowling at him. Julia began pacing.

'What shall we do?' she said.

We searched the rooms again. Nothing. Henry and Madeleine had disappeared.

✦✦✦

We stood around in Henry's dining room wondering what we should do. Our unfinished plates of cassoulet and half-filled wine glasses lay where we left them to search for Henry and Madeleine. Why would they suddenly take off like that? Why hadn't they returned?

We checked in the hall to see if Henry's coat was still there. It was impossible to tell. The coat rack was full and nobody knew how many coats Henry possessed. How could we know if one was missing? Martin offered to check the bedrooms again.

'Look under the beds,' I suggested.

'What?'

'You know what Henry's like. He could be playing one of his practical jokes.'

'Yes, but, under the beds?'

'Martin, just look everywhere.'

Carol was opening floor to ceiling cupboards in the utility area. Julia looked in the bathrooms.

John said, 'It's surprising how many places you could hide a body in your average house.'

I went back to the basement. I looked behind crates and boxes stacked against the walls in case Henry was playing a childish end of the world version of hide and seek. I wouldn't put it past him to deliberately give us a scare, especially on this last night of the Mayan calendar. He'd have a good old laugh afterwards about having watched us in secret, seeing how we coped with his sudden disappearance.

I returned to the dining room. Martin rushed in. He had a mobile phone in his hand.

'I found this on a nightstand,' he said. 'I think it's Henry's.'

'Scroll through his numbers,' I said. 'Madeleine's must be on there.'

He found it. Called it. We heard the sound of a ring tone: *Swan Lake*. We followed the sound to Henry's sitting room. There, on one of the sofas was an open handbag. Madeleine's phone was in its pouch. I grabbed it and looked at the readout: *Henry calling*. Another dead end.

Common sense told me he'd joined whoever the people were carrying lights up the mountain, but that didn't explain his mysterious departure without telling us, nor why Madeleine was missing as well. You'd have to be crazy to go climbing up the peak in the dark. I knew Henry was daft enough. But Madeleine? It didn't make sense.

In Henry's kitchen, the hob was left switched on, the pot still simmering.

'Anybody want some more cassoulet?' John said. 'We might as well help ourselves. I'm sure Henry wouldn't mind.'

He began slicing more bread. Only John, it seemed, still had an appetite. Martin scowled at him. The others looked puzzled, worried. Henry and Madeleine had disappeared from the party into the night and nobody knew what to do next. Carol was edgy, pulling at her hair and biting her lip.

'I don't know how you can stomach that,' she said as John dished another ladle full.

'Carol,' he said. 'They've gone up the mountain. It's obvious. Henry wouldn't want to miss out on that. The chance of seeing a buried spaceship? The mountain cracking wide open? He'd be first in line.'

'He wouldn't just leave without saying anything.'

I said, 'He might, if he was playing one of his tricks. We all know what he's like. Try not to worry.'

I could see she needed her husband. She wanted to be held, wanted to feel safe. John was at the table, eating greedily, oblivious to his wife's distress.

'Well, I'm going to make myself useful,' Julia said and began organising the removal of used plates, delegating duties to others and clearing things away in the kitchen. Carol glanced at me and joined her. Through the open kitchen door, I could hear them talking quietly.

'Ridiculous,' Julia was saying. 'Henry's completely out of order. You can't treat guests like this.'

'But, Julia, something might have happened to him.'

'I don't think so. I bet he's out there now, laughing at us. Making fools of all of us. You just don't do that to your friends.'

Carol said, 'Shall we make some coffee while we're waiting?'

They brought in a cafetière and a tray with enough cups for everybody. The others were milling about aimlessly, pacing past the glass doors, every now and then looking out to see if anything was happening out there in the dark. The lights we'd seen earlier had gone.

Martin suggested calling the police.

'No need,' I said. 'They're already here in Bugarach.'

John said, 'Do you think they left us any dessert?'

Carol's eyes looked watery. Her lips were trembling. Couldn't John see she needed comforting? He didn't know when to stop with the jokes, when to notice his wife, give her some attention, be there for her.

'You don't really think it's as serious as calling in the police, do you?' she said, her voice faltering.

John finished his second helping of cassoulet, took some coffee and said,

'Let's play a game.'

'You want to play a game?' Carol said. 'What's the matter with you?'

'A party game,' he said. 'It's a party isn't it? Henry would approve. He'd join in if he was here.'

Carol glared at him.

'You've had too much to drink,' she said.

Julia came to stand in the doorway and rolled her eyes. Martin and the others stopped their pacing and came to the table. Nobody else spoke.

'I'll start it,' John said. 'It's the truth game. You have to choose one thing you wish you'd done with your life and one thing you wish you hadn't.'

'John, stop it now,' Carol said.

'Come on, don't spoil it. It's the end of the world tonight folks. It's the only game to play.'

Nobody wanted to begin. John had the floor.

'I wish,' he said, 'I wish I'd started my own business when I had the opportunity.' He stared at his wife and added, 'and I wish I'd never moved to France.'

Carol hung her head.

'Your turn,' John said to her.

'I don't want to play,' she said.

'No. You never do. Somebody else, then? Anybody?'

Again, nobody volunteered. We sat and said nothing. It was plain to everybody except John we didn't want to join in. The others didn't even want to look at him; they kept their eyes turned away as if he might single out one of them and attempt to coerce them. I was about to suggest charades or some other pastime less involved, not so personally exposing, when Julia surprised me by saying,

'My turn. I wish I still had my husband. I wish he hadn't died.'

Oh, Julia, I thought. *John's going to make a meal out of you now.*

I closed my eyes. I could hardly bear to watch.

'Not admissible,' John said. 'Sorry, Julia, but that's not something where you had any choice to make.'

Don't say any more Julia.

'All right then,' she said. 'I wish I'd had a choice.'

'Still doesn't count,' John said. 'You'll have to think of something else. Oh, you can't can you? You never think about anything but your own loss.'

'John!' Carol shouted. 'That's enough.'

'I don't need you to defend me, Carol, thanks all the same,' Julia said. Her voice was calm but her eyes were on fire. She walked up to John and stood in front of him. I thought she was going to slap his face. I wouldn't have been surprised if she'd knocked him from his chair; he had asked for it.

'That was uncalled for,' she said to him. 'I could slap you to show you up, let people see what a thoughtless, immature bad mouth you can be, but I think you're making a good job of that all by yourself, John.'

The room went deathly quiet. Even John had nothing more to say.

'Some party this is turning out to be,' Martin said.

A young woman sitting beside Martin spoke up. She'd recently joined the choir. I didn't know her name.

'I will play,' she said. 'Is this what English people do at parties?'

Julia said, 'That's right. Tear each other to shreds.'

'Only when it's the end of the world,' John said.

'Very well. I wish I had learned to cook. Do I have to say the other thing?'

John nodded. He looked a little shame-faced. Maybe he was regretting what he'd started. Julia had gone to stand by the windows. She had her arms folded across her chest and, by the way she was taking deep slow breaths, I could tell she was doing her best to stay in control of her feelings.

'You don't have to continue,' Carol said. 'It's a stupid game, anyway.'

'But sometimes it is good for one to let out these things. Yes?' the girls said. 'I wish also that I had not given away my baby when I was seventeen. There, I have said it and now you all know the terrible thing I did.'

Martin stood up and all but thumped the table.

'I think this has gone far enough,' he said. 'We didn't come here for this. It's upsetting my wife.' The woman on his right had a handkerchief to her nose. 'Janice, I'll get your coat.'

'You can't leave now,' Carol said. 'What about Henry and Madeleine?'

'They'll be fine,' John said. 'Why do you always have to make such a big thing out of everything?'

'Probably because she's married to *you*,' Julia said.

Carol looked at me, her eyes pleading me to intervene.

'We don't know they'll be all right,' she said. 'They could be out there now in the dark, needing our help.'

'Look,' I said. 'We'll give it another hour and if they're not back by then, I'll go down to the village and let the police know what's happened. Julia can come with me to explain.'

'And then we can go home,' Julia added. 'I've had enough of all this nonsense.'

The others left. There was no point in everybody hanging on, they said. We're tired, they said. We've got a long drive home. Let us know the outcome, they said. We hope everything turns out all right. See you in the New Year.

The young woman with Martin and his wife hung back from the others to apologise for leaving. She said she had a lift home with Martin and Janice and must go with them. I felt she was the one who deserved an apology.

'I'm sorry, too.' I said.

'Did I say something wrong in the truth game?' she asked me.

'No.'

'But the party has ended as soon as I spoke. Now I am, how do you say? Embarrassed.'

'I don't know your name. Now I'm embarrassed.'

'Luisa.'

'You're French?'

'Spanish.'

Martin came in with her coat. He hurried her out of the house. I stood at the top of Henry's steps and watched the seven of them holding hands or linking arms in the darkness, shuffling down the hill toward the village. Only Luisa turned to look back.

'I don't know how any of them could sleep tonight not knowing what's happened to Henry,' Carol said when they'd gone.

'Oh, it's surprising what one can learn to cope with,' Julia said, her voice as quiet as it was bitter. She pulled on the drapes in the dining room to shut out the night. John was in the kitchen searching through Henry's fridge for desserts.

'Here they are, look,' he called. 'I knew there would be something somewhere.'

He helped himself, brought a portion to the table and sat to eat.

'What?' he said when he saw the three of us watching him. 'When Henry comes back through that door, you'll all have some.'

I turned my head away.

There were no more lights on the mountain. We heard no more mysterious humming. The land was quiet. Henry's house stood by the silent lake above the village, at the foot of the mountain as it had for hundreds of years. The rocks didn't open up and the world didn't end and the hour passed. I put on my coat.

'Julia?' I said.

'I'm coming.'

Carol reached out to touch my arm. Her eyes were full of longing, her mouth soft and inviting.

'Be careful,' she said.

Julia said, 'Oh, for goodness' sake.'

Carol withdrew her hand quickly, but beside his wife, John finally noticed the way she'd looked at me.

Julia and I walked carefully in the light from my mobile, picking our way in the darkness, past the lake and through the heath, following the stony path down the hill. My sister held tightly to my arm. Neither of us spoke. Soon, the lights of Bugarach came into view and I felt Julia's grip slacken.

'Ridiculous,' she said under her breath. I wasn't certain which part of the night's proceedings she was referring to. Maybe she meant all of it.

The village was still in party mood, music and laughter everywhere, doors thrown open and people milling about from house to house.

'It's a pity they haven't got something better to do,' Julia said.

My stomach lurched. Months of keeping the peace with her in our shared home curdled inside me like something gone rotten. Together with the bad feeling John had caused, I felt as if my energies had expired, as if they'd been sucked out of me. My patience evaporated. My face grew hot. My mouth tasted sour.

'Julia,' I said. 'They're just having fun. Remember *fun*, sister dear?'

She sniffed and drew herself up.

She said, 'You mean like John's ridiculous parlour game? You call that fun?'

'No,' I said. 'I don't. He went too far. He'd had too much to drink. I'm not talking about John. He's an angry man; that's his problem. I'm talking about us. About the way we used to be. We used to laugh, Julia. What happened? You've forgotten how to laugh. You're always so . . . critical.'

'Don't you dare speak to me like that.'

She moved to hurry on ahead of me, but I grabbed her arm.

'Somebody has to tell you,' I said. 'It's better if it comes from me.'

She tried to shake me off, but I held onto her. 'Please, listen to me. I want you to understand what I'm trying to say. We all know you've been grieving. We know you've been hurting. But there was some truth in what John said tonight. It was cruel the way he said it, but honestly, Julia you're not yourself any more.'

She stopped and stared at me. Under the streetlight her eyes were cold and empty. Her mouth turned down; briefly, her whole face sagged. She looked at me as if I'd just stabbed her. Then, she gathered herself, lifted her chin and cocked her head.

'How could I be?' she said. 'How could I be myself? How can I ever be happy again?'

She was using *that* voice again. It was coming out of the patronising headmistress face. I snapped.

'You don't have to take it out on other people.' The words had slipped out. It wasn't what I meant to say, what I should have said. Her lips clamped tight together and she turned her back on me. She strode off toward the village centre.

'Julia!' I shouted. 'Julia, I'm sorry.'

I ran after her and caught up. 'Please, Julia. Don't walk off like that. I'm sorry if I hurt you.'

My stomach was tight and burning. Half of me wanted to make everything right with my sister and the other half simply wanted to get away, be free of it. I walked beside her as she hurried along the main street. I don't remember what else I said as I scuttled along at her side. She was staring straight ahead and wouldn't answer me.

I saw the gendarme we'd spoken to earlier. He was in a casual sweater, smoking roll-ups and drinking coffee with a noisy group spilling out of the bar. Aliens had taken off their headdresses and were swigging beer from bottles, laughing high priestesses and fortune tellers draped around them, hanging on their arms. They waved at us. Julia carried on walking.

'Where are you going?' I said.

'Home. I've got the car keys in my bag. You can get a lift with *Carol*.'

'I thought you were going to speak to the police.'

'Do it yourself.'

I watched her walk away. Guilt mixed with relief made my head swim. I was sorry I'd upset her, but at the same time had a sense of release that finally I'd said what I felt. Surely, she would understand. Wouldn't she see I meant it for the best?

She marched away from me, stepping down the street like the strict headmistress, head up, shoulders back. Imperious again. I saw stiff pride in her straight back and the way she held her head. She strode out, angry, determined. In a way, I was glad of it, glad for *her*. It meant that at least for now, she wasn't grieving. She'd stopped thinking about her loss. She was angry with me instead. Maybe now she'd be able to move on.

Perhaps I'd said the right thing in the wrong way. I couldn't unsay it. I hoped she'd find a way through her anger, her sorrow and rediscover the sister she used to be. I missed her, my sister-mum who used to be gentle and kind, the one who got me out of scrapes at school, the one who saved sweets for me, let me have the biggest piece of chocolate cake. I'd come to the end of the road with the Julia I was living with, her constant criticism, her overbearing manner. That sister was squeezing the life out of me, squashing me flat.

She disappeared around the corner and I knew in that instant our own small world was changing, coming to an end. I didn't want her dependence on me any longer. I hoped she'd find the strength to let me go.

I walked back up the rise toward the table outside the bar where the gendarme was sitting with end of the world revellers. The door to the interior stood open. Golden light spilled out onto the stones, shining in a gilded pool by the entrance.

Another group of Martians and monsters came outside to join their friends. They carried plates of sugary doughnuts. Their sweet, greasy smell wafted on the air. Happy music filled the street. There was laughter and the sound of glasses chinking. One of the Martians grabbed a high priestess and pulled her into an exaggerated Hollywood-style clinch. He stuffed a piece of doughnut into her open, willing mouth and she responded with much smacking of lips and more laughter.

I had serious news to bring. I would be the cause of the end of their fun. Two people were missing and it was time to stop the party. First, I had to find the right vocabulary to speak to the gendarme. It occurred to me then, that if Julia had depended on me in many ways over the years, it was also true I had depended on her.

I hadn't a clue how to explain in French about the disappearance of Henry and Madeleine.

✦✦✦

I stood in the street outside the bar in Bugarach and didn't know where to begin. The end of the world party was still in full swing and I was like a beggar at the feast, the harbinger of grim news. I couldn't begin to explain what had happened at Henry's house. My French was limited, mostly in the present tense and amounted to ordering food and drink, no thank you and have a nice day. Realising just how much I'd depended on Julia was like a slap in the face.

I'd always stood back and let her deal with everything: making appointments at the dentist, talking to mechanics when it was time for my car's *Controle Technique*, the French version of an MOT and filling in tax forms. I'd expected Julia to deal with every bit of French officialdom and she'd done it without complaint. I'd made little, if any, effort to improve my schoolboy French and now, here I was, hoping to explain to the gendarme outside the bar that my good friend Henry and his lady friend had disappeared and been missing for over two hours.

Anything could have happened in that time. I should have paid more attention to what Carol said. She'd been the only one who'd shown an appropriate degree of concern. The rest of us had been content to put their disappearance down to Henry's love of playing practical jokes. Supposing one of them had fallen and the other was still trying to get them both off the mountain? What if there were broken bones, or worse?

Stop supposing, I thought. *Get on with what you have to do.*

But, where to begin? I felt inadequate and foolish. I was like a child again, hoping somebody was going to come along and deal with the difficult stuff for me. I saw myself in the playing fields behind our house where the little kids used the swings and bigger kids hung around. I'd be crying over a spilled packet of crisps and suddenly, there would be Julia rushing through the gap in our fence, galloping in like the cavalry, tidying up the mess I'd made and giving me a consolation biscuit.

Oh, Julia, I'm so sorry I hurt you, I thought. *I've made a mess of things. Again. Why have I been looking at only your faults and ignoring my own?*

Wasn't I Camilla Rose? The man who understood women? The man who wrote about their feelings? It seemed recognising how a woman was feeling was one thing: knowing what to do about it was something very different. Would Julia ever forgive me?

I stepped forward and caught the gendarme's attention. He put down his drink and raised his eyebrows.

'How may I help you?' he said.

I didn't understand every word. Languedoc pronunciation varies from perceived French: its roots are in an older language, Occitan, but from the questioning look in his eyes and the tilt of his head, I got the gist of his question. I coughed and felt ridiculous, *Julia's word*. The aliens and female monsters sitting with him all stared at me.

'It is my friend,' I said. 'I am looking for my friend. *Je cherche Henri*. He has disappeared. *Henri a disparu.*'

I knew my accent sounded terrible.

' 'Enri Gallois?' he said. 'Yes, I have seen him. He is inside.'

'What? I mean, *repetez, s'il vous plait.*'

'He is here,' the gendarme said, indicating the bar. '*Dedans*. He is inside.'

' 'Enri Gallois. 'Enri Gallois,' the silver and green-faced aliens chanted. They got up and began an inebriated stomping dance around the table.

' 'Enri Gallois, 'Enri Gallois,' they said again and added in English, ' 'Enri the Welsh, where are you?'

I thanked them all. One offered me a doughnut. For politeness' sake, I took it. I said thank you again. I went inside.

The bar was crowded with people in long robes and carnival costume, jesters and masked harlequins and medieval maidens with elaborate hairpieces, others dressed as astronauts and more aliens and a rather out of place Father Christmas. The room sounded like a wasps' nest, the buzz of conversations vibrating against the bar's pulsing background music.

As I pushed my way through the throng, someone stole the doughnut from my hand. I heard French and English and something else I couldn't decipher, probably the woman called Sylvie speaking the language as yet unknown on Earth. The no smoking rule had been abandoned for the night. The air was thick with smoke, not all of it tobacco. No wonder the gendarme chose to stay outside. Indoors, there'd be too many people to arrest. The resulting paperwork would take months.

I found Henry up at the bar, smoking one of his special occasion cigars. Madeleine was with him. A raucous crowd of revellers was buying drinks: more aliens and characters from *Star Wars*, robots and androids and Sylvie of the feathery hat. Henry had three glasses lined up on the bar beside him. He grinned when he saw me. He was already spaced.

'Couldn't get away,' he said, leaning forward to shake my hand and almost falling from his bar stool. 'Sorry. Everything all right?'

My relief to see him safe gave way to anger.

'The ladies were worried about you, Henry,' I said.

'Does that mean you weren't bothered at all?'

He reached out to pick up a glass and nearly knocked it flying.

'Henry,' I said. 'We didn't know what had happened to you.'

'Well, here I am and all is well.'

'You should have let us know where you were going,' I said and winced because I sounded like Julia.

He threw an arm around Madeleine's shoulder.

'Meet my wife,' he said.

'Your *wife*?'

Madeleine nodded and smiled.

Henry said, 'As from tonight, my wife. We were going to make a surprise announcement before we left the house, but this lot were waiting outside. See him over there?'

He pointed to Father Christmas. "That is the mayor of Bugarach. He married us under the stars. Lovely ceremony we had, up there on the side of the mountain.'

It all began to fall into place. Now I understood the snatched glances at one another and my feeling they were hiding a secret.

I said, 'We saw the lights.'

'Beautiful, it was. A choir of angels singing to the heavens.'

That explained the humming noises.

'So you had it all planned? Another of your little tricks, Henry?'

'That's right.'

'Even the power cut?'

'No, no. That was nothing to do with me. It's a regular occurrence. I was going to nip back inside and tell you about the candlelight procession, invite you all up there, but the buggers grabbed us and marched us off to get married. Anyway, I got the power back on straight away.'

'No, Henry. The lights stayed out.'

'Did they? Well, there you are then. I tell you now, it's always happening.'

He pulled his new wife in close to him and planted a drunken kiss on her head.

'Magnetic forces,' he said. 'Magnetic forces. You can't resist 'em, you know. Stay and have a drink with us.'

'Henry,' I said. 'You must have passed the house on your way down here. Couldn't you have let us know then?'

Madeleine intervened.

'I'm sorry,' she said. 'I can see how it must look. We thought you would see us coming back down the hill and come out to join in.'

I remembered Julia had pulled on the curtains in Henry's dining room. We hadn't seen the returning procession. In any case, we'd all been too busy searching through the house to notice what was happening outside.

Henry said, 'Come on, Paul. You're here now. All's well that ends well. Have a drink. Call thc others and get them down here.'

'Most of them have gone home.'

'Not all that worried then, were they?'

I stayed. I sent a text to John's mobile to let them know where I was and that Henry and Madeleine were safe. I didn't mention the mountainside wedding. Didn't want to steal Henry's thunder. He enjoyed surprising people. I could imagine Carol's face when Henry explained what had really happened on the night of the end of the world. She'd probably shed a tear. John wouldn't notice.

A few minutes later, my phone rattled its text alert. The reply was from Carol.

Glad ur ok. Going home now. C you.

I texted back.

Let Julia know. I'm staying here.

Knowing that everything was fine would be one less thing for my sister to worry about. It was the least I could do, even if I couldn't face talking to her myself just then. I turned off my phone and put it in my pocket. I wanted no more calls. Wanted the unavailability. I needed to forget the argument with Julia, relax and enjoy myself. I looked at the crowd of end of the world partygoers and wanted to be like them, carousing, not thinking about a thing, making lots of noise.

I hoped John and Carol wouldn't change their minds and come to find me. I positioned myself where I could see through the crowd and out into the street. I kept glancing out. I saw them pass by. They were walking apart from one another, Carol muffled in a wide wrap around her shoulders, John with his hands stuffed inside his pockets. I guessed there was a lot of talking for them to do later. I leaned back against the bar and let my lift home go without me.

Henry was ploughing his way through drinks lined up on the bar. Madeleine was curled in a sofa by the wall, deep in conversation with Sylvie.

'You'd better help me with these, Paul,' Henry said, indicating his queue of drinks. 'Got to admit defeat. Don't want to get completely ratted. It's my wedding night, you know.'

He glanced at his bride and pulled a face like the kid who's just grabbed the last chocolate biscuit. You can't stay angry with Henry for long.

'I'm looking for a place to sleep tonight, Henry,' I said. 'How are you fixed?'

'You can have one of the sofas. We filled the bedrooms with this lot.'

The wedding breakfast at three am at Henry's was an inter-galactic affair. Henry and Madeleine moved among silver suited and booted aliens, high priestesses and the rest, handing out bacon rolls and soya burgers. Sylvie had cast off her feathery hat and was now speaking perfect English.

'A thousand euro,' she was telling somebody in a Batman outfit. 'That's what I heard. A thousand a night. They'll be able to winter in the Caribbean on the proceeds.'

I didn't hear who *they* were, but I gathered that Bugarach homeowners had been coining it in, renting out their spare rooms and charging three hundred a day to pitch tents in their gardens. Now, the fateful night had passed and Henry's guests were discussing plans for their next gathering. Henry came and put his hand on my shoulder.

'Come with me,' he said. 'It's too noisy in here.'

I followed him into the sitting room. Madeleine joined us. Henry closed the door and sat beside me.

'You don't have to tell me anything, old boy,' he said, 'but if you need a place to stay, you can house sit for us. We're leaving tomorrow.'

'Honeymoon,' Madeleine said and I swear Henry actually looked bashful. 'You're welcome to stay here, Paul. It's very peaceful. Perhaps you'd be able to get on with some writing.'

'Where are you going?' I said.

Henry said, 'Mexico. On a mission. We're scouting out the next end of the world.'

I think he was joking. He got up. From the bookshelf he took a crystal skull and bounced it in his palm.

'Those things are mass produced in Vietnam, Henry,' I said.

He laughed.

'Did you think I didn't know that?' he said.

Madeleine leaned over and gently touched the back of my hand.

'Stay here and get well,' she said. 'Play music. Read. Relax.'

'If you run us to the airport,' Henry said, 'you can have the use of the car while we're gone. Keep it ticking over and all that.'

My eyelids were drooping. Their voices were fading. It was an effort to respond to their suggestions.

The next thing I knew, Madeleine was gently shaking my shoulder. Daylight lit the sitting room. Someone had thrown a duvet over me and put a pillow under my head. I blinked and rubbed my eyes.

'Sorry to wake you,' Henry said, 'But we've got to make tracks soon. Check in is at four thirty.'

Madeleine said she'd made coffee and I went to use the bathroom. Their suitcases were in the hall. I thought about Julia and her argument with John. I remembered the way Carol had looked at me and held onto my hand. It seemed like a good idea to stay at Henry's, keep out of the way of everybody and let things settle.

'So, you'll stay?' Madeleine said as I joined them in the kitchen and helped myself to croissants.

'Yes. Thank you both. I'd like that very much.' I scooped a spoon of jam.

'Get rid of the others, will you?' Henry said, nodding toward the ceiling. 'There are bodies all over the place upstairs. The house looks like a scene from a disaster movie. Tell them I'll be in touch when we get back.'

'Will do.'

Madeleine was humming quietly as she cleared things away.

'I enjoyed your song last night,' I said.

'Wonderful, isn't she?' Henry said, beaming from ear to ear. 'Could have been in opera, you know.'

'No, Henry,' she said. 'I wasn't cut out for it in the end.'

'So, you were trained?'

'Yes. It's what I thought I wanted to do with my life. But life had other plans.'

'What happened?'

'I had a good voice, but not a *great* one, Paul,' she said. 'And now I'm going to let you into a secret, a failing of mine.'

'Not what I'd call a failing,' Henry said.

'A weakness then. It wouldn't have made any difference how well my voice was trained. I don't have the *performance* temperament. You must have that if you want to be the best.'

'And you wanted to be the best?' I said.

'Yes. Nerves let me down. You have to believe in yourself if you want to give a great performance.'

Beautiful, confident Madeleine had secret fears?

'But, you sang beautifully last night,' I said.

'That's different. I was among friends. Not quite the same feeling in the grand opera houses with vast spaces and thousands of eyes on you. But, I knew I couldn't give up music altogether.'

'You teach?' I said.

'I'm a therapist. I switched career and began a very different course of study, but I use music in my work. We're doing great things at the moment helping people with neurological disease.'

I wanted to learn more. Madeleine's work sounded fascinating, but Henry looked at his watch.

'Maddy, we really must get a move on.'

I saw them off at the airport for their flight to Paris and connection onwards. They looked like teenagers again setting out on an adventure. Through the glass panes separating the small departure lounge from the boarding gates, I could see them laughing as they went through security, taking off their shoes and belts and jewellery, getting in a muddle and falling over one another. I envied them that happiness. They turned and waved before they disappeared from view.

I drove slowly on the way back. The December afternoon was mild and I cruised like a Sunday driver, taking in the scenery and enjoying quiet country lanes. Staying at Henry's place on my own was going to be a new experience. I looked forward to the novelty. Without Julia I'd have to practise my French.

The approach to Henry's farmhouse takes a longer route than the footpath we'd used the day before. It bypasses the village centre and winds its way upward, cutting through forest and comes out beside the lake. As I neared the house, I saw lights at the door and activity out front where two cars were parked.

'Hello,' Sylvie called as I got out of Henry's four by four. 'We're just packing up, ready to leave. Did they get off okay?'

'Yes,' I said. 'Fine.'

'I'm so happy for them,' she said. She took my arms and kissed me on the cheek. 'Glad you're back. We didn't like to leave the house unlocked, although I don't suppose that matters much up here. So nice to meet you. Perhaps we'll meet again.'

Two men and three women came out and joined her, but I didn't recognise any of them minus green faces and weird clothes. They bundled in their belongings and drove off, hooting, their car headlights making cone shapes up and down as they bounced over ruts in the track.

I made a hot drink and a sandwich and sat on Henry's front doorstep watching night fall. The lake turned silver. A breeze rippled the surface. The smell of moist winter earth drifted on the air. I breathed in deeply and the breath became a yawn. My bones ached. I was exhausted.

I used the spare room at the back of the house as Madeleine had suggested. She'd kindly left out clean bed linen and fresh towels on a chest. I made up the bed and took a shower. As I sank into the soft bed I reflected on the previous day's events. From where I lay next to the window, I could see the night sky full of silent stars. The house was still and quiet.

I wondered how far into their journey the newly married couple had travelled. They'd looked so at ease, so happy together. I'd forgotten what it was like to look with love into the eyes of a woman and see that love reflected in her own gaze. I wrote about it, but that was as close as I got. Since the split with my ex there'd been no special woman in my life. I'd convinced myself it was never going to happen again. That part of me didn't exist any more. It was shut off, closed down, perished like old rubber.

I was glad John had finally sensed how Carol was slipping away from him. I would only have hurt her. In the end, I would have had to tell her my feelings for her didn't match hers for me. It occurred to me how clearly you can see other people's problems but remain ignorant of the roots of your own. Maybe for John and Carol it wasn't too late to mend it.

Henry's guest bed was comfortable, but I lay there waiting for sleep. Although I was exhausted my mind wouldn't stop. Ideas for stories thrust themselves at me. I got out of bed and searched for pen and paper. I found a notepad downstairs by the telephone.

I needed to get back to work, fill my life with things I enjoyed. I had let things drift too long. I would stay in Bugarach till Madeleine and Henry returned. Then, it would be time to start afresh, make decisions.

✦✦✦

I woke and didn't know what day it was. Saturday? Sunday? How long had I slept? Was it yesterday I'd slept on Henry's sofa, or the day before?

I sat on the edge of the bed and looked out the window. The peak behind Henry's farmhouse was shrouded in grey mist. Fine drizzle spattered on the glass. My head hurt. My neck ached and my shoulders felt stiff. I dressed quickly and went downstairs.

The house was cold. I put on my coat and went to collect logs from the basement. I stacked them in the space by the log burner in Henry's living room. I made enough trips to fill the alcove and the basket. I found firelighters and set it alight. It was soon blazing, but I still felt cold.

Food and drink. That's what I need, I thought. I sat by the fire with a reheated burger in a toasted roll and coffee. My whole body ached. My legs felt heavy and my eyes hurt. I switched on television but couldn't concentrate on anything. When I stood to go to the bathroom, my legs wobbled and I almost fell.

I really don't need this now. Please, no. Not the flu. The room swam and I felt sick. I only just made it to the downstairs bathroom in time.

I spent the next three days wrapped in a duvet on a sofa in the sitting room by the fire. The walk to the kettle was easier from there. The bedroom was too chilly and the stairs too much of an effort. I dozed through Christmas films and television comedy specials, only moving from the sofa to throw on a couple more logs or to make another hot drink. I didn't hear from Julia. I hoped she was feeling better than I did.

Stay here and get well, Madeleine had said to me. Had I looked ill even then? I examined my face in the bathroom mirror: dark circles under my eyes, queer skin colour. I remembered something Julia used to say.

Teachers always fall ill during school holidays, she'd tell me.

It went along the lines of adrenaline keeping you going through the stress. Then, as soon as you relaxed, you went under. Was that what had happened to me? Had I been under stress without realising it? Was it as a result of living with Julia and feeling resentful? Missing who she used to be?

Christmas came and went. As soon as I felt well enough, I went out. I walked the path around the lake, trekked through forest and watched birds of prey hovering in thermals near the mountain. The winter sky was the colour of gentians. Tepid December sun lit the resting land. Ideas for new novels flooded in. Walking always helped me see things in a different light.

When I returned to Henry's house, I knew what I had to do. I picked up the phone. It wasn't too late for me to make a fresh start.

Henry and Madeleine had showed me that. Sometimes you just have to accept that things are not working out and before you can move on to the new, you have to set the old things free.

Julia wasn't surprised when I told her my plans did not include her.

HE*ARSE from Wikipedia*
a vehicle used to carry a coffin from a church or funeral home to a cemetery

SOMETHING TO SAY

Unconsecrated ground, that is, Deirdre. All them plots up there at the top. Unconsecrated. Well, that'd be about right for him, wouldn't it, love? Can't go mixing up the faiths, can they?

Yes, it is a bit steep, Deirdre. It's a fair old pull up this hill. Mind how you go. Watch that puddle.

Never had a religion, did he? Never had much faith in anything, really. Did everything his own way. Not a religious bone in his body. The only time I ever heard a reference to the Bible coming out of his mouth was when he was swearing. Ah, yes, you're right. Or when he was drunk. Watch that dog shit, Deirdre.

Yes, it is a bit steep. Yes, it is a bit of a climb. Not as nimble as we used to be, are we? If you like we can stop. We'll sit on this bench, love. Just for a breather. That's right, Deirdre love. Sit yerself down. We can catch up in a minute. Put yer bag here, love. Mind yer leg. Right? Settled? That's better. Just take a breather.

Eeeh, that's a grand view, that is. Look at that view, Deirdre. All that sky. All them Yorkshire hills. What a place to spend eternity, eh? Right up here on the tops looking down at that lot. Bloody cold in winter, though. Cuts you in half, the wind up here.

See that over there? That's Lister's Mill. Look. You can recognise them chimneys from miles away. That's where I first met him, you know. He used to be the overlooker in the twisting and folding. All the girls had a soft spot for him then. Oh, but you knew that anyway.

You're right, love. Times were different then. Yes, we were all busy. Jobs everywhere. You could walk out of one job in the morning and get set on in a new onc by the afternoon. The whole bloody place was so busy growing we didn't notice we were all getting older. You're right, love. It were no age. Sixty- four. No age at all. Never even collected his first pension, did he, love?

Oh, bloody Nora, look who's coming. No, don't look now Deirdre. It's Jack bloody Sprat and 'er. No, well I know that's not his real name, Deirdre. Right bloody tight-arse, that one. Always last to buy a round in. And 'er? Lady bloody Docker? Huh. I could tell a few tales about 'er an' all. Used to be the local bike, she did. Ice cream lady at the Ritz. That's all she was.

Hello, Jack. Eva, love. Keeping well? No, we're fine, thank you. Deirdre's leg playing up. That's all. We'll be up in a minute.

Jesus, Deirdre. Did you see that coat? Did you see the state of it? It's had more outings than Anderton's bloody coach trips, has that fake fur. They'll have to bury 'er in that bloody coat.

Yes, love, I know. In his favourite Elvis costume. Spangles and everything. And the wig. Well, he has no more use for it now down here, love. He'll be up there entertaining St. Peter and the angels. Eeeh, I used to love it when he did Jailhouse Rock. Well, when he were younger, like. 'Appen it'll be 'The Old Rugged Cross' from now on, eh?

There's a fair few turned out for him. I'll say that. Yes, love, we're at that age now. The only time we get to see the old crowd is when we're planting one of us. Did you go to Pauline's last month at the Crem? Did you not? Heartbreaking it were, Deirdre.

Heartbreaking. All the grandkids lined up in a long row, each with a single rose. Even that weird one. Whatsisname? Liam. That's him. I'll tell you. There's summat not quite right about that one. We'll be reading about him one day in the Sunday Mirror.

Are you ready to move on now? Come on, then. Don't forget yer bag. Mind yer leg. Yes, it is a bit steep, Deirdre. Take me arm. Here, look. Grab hold. That's it. Nearly there. Just a few more steps.

Is that Brighouse Bob over there having a fag? Nay, Bob, you should have a bit more respect. I said Bob, Deirdre. You know, from Brighouse. Brighouse Bob. Used to play slide trombone in the Brighouse and Raistrick until he lost his puff. Well, we know why now, don't we? Is it not? Isn't it him? I forgot me glasses. I've only got me readers with me. For reading menu later. Oh yes, I expect there'll be menus. It's a sit-down do, not a boofay. There's always menus at a sit-down do.

Yes, it is a bit steep, Deirdre. Mind how you go. Is this the plot? Is this it, here? Well, bugger me. That's my Ken right behind him. Fancy that. Who'd have thought, eh? Back to back. Ken and Barry. They never did see eye to eye, did they, Deirdre? Could never agree on anything. And now, here they'll be. Head to head. Forever. What a turn up. Somebody upstairs is having a joke with us, Deirdre.

Yes, love it's fitting. It's damp and miserable. Very fitting for a funeral. But still, it could be worse. It's a bloody nightmare getting up here in the winter. I say to my Ken, I say 'Goodbye love. See you in the spring.' Yes love. Round about October. Well, it's too much of an effort after then. The wind whips round them hills and down through this valley, fit to knock you over. The rain comes sideways at you and when it snows, you can't get up here anyway. Not unless you've got a bloody tractor. You'll see.

That's Frank Wilson at the back there, look, Deirdre. Is that his daughter he's brought with him? Her with the spiky heels and too much make-up. Well, I knew he'd got married again, Deirdre. And that's her, is it? Bloody hell. He must have found that one in a catalogue. Hey, I bet she can sing. Legs like a canary.

And there's little Julie, look. Do you remember, Deirdre, when Barry used to sing for her in the tap room at the Hope and Anchor? All them oldies. Julie, Julie, Julie do ya love me? Julie, Julie, Julie, do ya care? And she'd sit there gazing at him with that stupid look on her face. You what, love? Yes, you're right, Deirdre. All water under the bridge now.

I can't see David from the Burlington Arms. No, I can't see him anywhere. Well, I thought he'd have made the effort, Deirdre. I did really. Barry helped him out a time or two, didn't he? David from the Burlington Arms. Kept pigeons round the back. Had whippets an' all. Shitting and pissing everywhere. I'd have thought he coulda made the effort to show his face. I'll be having a word with him when I see him.

Now then, I know this minister. I thought I recognised him back there at the chapel. Yes, I know who he is. Oh, I'm right glad it's him, Deirdre. He's a lovely lad. His mother used to have one of them posh flats at the Aire Valley. Went to live in Spain with her fancy man. Years younger than her, he was. Well, you know what they say, love. They don't look at the mantelpiece when they're poking the fire.

But he's a lovely lad, though. Hasn't he got a lovely voice, Deirdre? Like dark chocolate. It goes right through you. Look at his hands. Expressive. That's what they call hands like that, Deirdre. Expressive. He looks like a young Jesus, don't you think?

You know, how we all imagine a young Jesus. I didn't know they were allowed to have long hair like that. Did you?

Now don't take on, Deirdre. It's finished now. That's it now. All done. I thought it were a nice touch, though. Playing that music for him as they lowered him in. Was that one of his favourites? Return to Sender? No, don't take on, Deirdre. Come on, love. Let's make a move. Get back to the cars. We don't want to be last ones into Wagon and Horses. Take me arm, Deirdre. That's it.

Yes, it is a bit steep, Deirdre. Yes, it is a bit worse going back down again. Is it your leg again, love? Do you want to stop? We can sit here again and watch 'em coming down. Have another look at that raggy-arsed fake fur. No? You're sure? Come on then, let's keep going.

No, that's not true, Deirdre, love. You're not on yer own. You have got somebody left. You've got me, Deirdre. We've got each other. That's who we've got now, Deirdre. Each other. Don't you worry about that.

No, love. Cars'll wait. They won't go without you, love. And it won't matter if we are last ones in to pub. They won't start serving till you get there. I'll have something to say if they do. That'd be out of order, that would. You're his widow, love. We've all come to say goodbye to Barry but it's you we've come to support.

Mind that pothole, Deirdre. Yes, it is a bit steep. Did you say you were having an open bar, love? Just for first drinks, is it?

Here we are, Deirdre. This is you. This is your car, love. Leading car's for nearest and dearest. Mind yer leg. Have you got yer bag? Hang on a minute driver! She's got her coat jammed in the door. Are you all right, Deirdre, love? Right then, I'll be five minutes behind you. That's all. Don't you worry about that. See you there. Oh, Deirdre, I'll have a large whisky.

Hello, Julie. Are you by yourself? Oh, I'm sorry to hear that. Tell him I hope he's better soon. I'll catch up with you later. I don't want to leave Deirdre too long on her own. You know how it is.

No, she's bearing up, Julie, love. Well, you have to, don't you? What else can you do? You have to keep going, don't you? Life goes on for us that's left. Oh, you're right, Julie. We have no say in it. We don't get to choose which of us goes first. The only thing we can be sure about is that one of us will. Be first to go.

Are you not going on to Wagon and Horses? Oh, what a shame. Deirdre was just saying she remembered how much you used to like Barry's singing. Aye, we all did. Nice memories, eh, love? Well, think on. Remember me to Billy, won't you, Julie love?

Eva, love! Are you and Jack going on? Have you got space for a little one? Only, Deirdre forgot to book me into one of the laid-on cars. Yes, she's all over the place. Can't concentrate on anything at the moment. Well, it's to be expected. Yes, I know. Terrible. So sudden. No age at all. Poor bugger. Never got to enjoy retirement.

But you've got to keep going, haven't you, love? She'll learn. It's hard when you're on yer own, but she'll learn. It's these first few weeks hit you hardest. Well, it's like none of it's real. And then the first birthday. The first Christmas. The first anniversary. Then when it comes to the second time round, it's not quite so bad as the first year, and you wake up one morning and think, 'well, I'm still here so I might as well get on with it'.

In the back here, Jack? Oh, Eva, this is a lovely car. You know the way there, don't you? That's right. No, it's a sit-down do. That's what Deirdre wanted. Like I said, she's all over the place.

I'll be there for her, though. I'll stick by her. I won't let her be on her own. She's got me.

It's not easy just now, Eva. No, it's not. Yes, you've got to mind what you say to the newly bereaved. Did she tell you it's open bar? Just for first drinks. Make sure you don't miss out, Jack.

***

THE END

ABOUT THE AUTHOR

Celia Micklefield has worked in an accountant's office, a high street retail chain store, a textile mill and a shoe factory as well as short stints in a fish and chip shop, behind the bar in a pub and running a slimming club. She studied for a teaching degree and went into teaching at high school, became a partner in an import and wholesale business and ran a craft outlet at a country shopping experience. She returned to teaching where her last position was at a sixth form college.

She was born in West Yorkshire and has lived in Aberdeenshire and Norfolk. Now she lives in southern France.

Celia has a website at www.celiamicklefield.com where she regularly blogs her Random Thoughts. She also keeps a Celia Micklefield Facebook page.

Printed in Great Britain
by Amazon